About the Author

Lexie Winston has been an astronaut, rock star, princess and time traveller. In her dreams. But none of the dreams have lived up to what becoming an author has been like. She gets to live in a world of pure imagination, and her heroines get to do the things she's always wished she could.

When not writing books, Lexie is a mother of two gorgeous teenagers and the wife to a patient and understanding man. They live in Western Australia and are lorded over by a black toy poodle. She loves camping, reading and if her iPad was stolen, her world would explode. (It has the kindle app on it.)

And you can find all my links at

www.lexiewinston.com

The Collectors Division

(Paranormal Reverse Harem Series)

Guardian

Guardian's Blood

Guardian Ascending

Collector's Division Omnibus

Neighpalm Industries Collective

(Enemies to Lovers Reverse Harem)

Abandoned Girl

Broken Girl

Tormented Girl

Wanted Girl

Cherished Girl

Loved Girl

Superficial Girl - Jacinta's Story Part 1

Superficial Girl - Jacinta's Story Part 2

Neighpalm Industries Collective 1-3

Neighpalm Industries Collective 4-6

Seductive Sins Collection

(Reverse Harem Series)

Glorious Gluttony

Gangs, Guns, and Glory

Galaxy Circus

(Sci-Fi Reverse Harem Series)

Apprentice

Stagehand

Whisperer

Mama - Galaxy Circus Novella

Performer

A Night Most Wicked - Galaxy Circus Novella

Broken Promises

(Dark Poly Romance Series)

Secrets Kept

Lies Untold

Trust Broken

Love Found

M.I.T.H.O.S

(Contemporary RH)

Spies Like Me

GLORIOUS GLUTTONY

LEXIE WINSTON

First published by Neighpalm Publishing in 2020

Glorious Gluttony
Mobi format: 978-0-6487006-3-0
Print: 978-0-6487006-6-1

Cover design by Lexie Winston
Edited by Pen and Ink editing
Proofread by Locke and Key Proofreading

 Created with Vellum

*For food lovers everywhere. Don't ever be ashamed of liking
what you like*

Chapter One

"Miss! Excuse me, miss!"

I walk a little faster toward my table, the click-clack of her shoes echoing behind me. Good, she's wearing high heels. I might just get away.

Smirking, I pick up the pace, feeling my butt cheeks jiggling in my skirt like a dancing hippopotamus. I try carefully not to spill the plate I'm carrying while I make my escape. I look back. The woman is still following me, and she, too, has picked up the pace.

It's not easy weaving in and out of the tables at top speed, and the senior citizens dotted throughout the room make the journey even more perilous. I mean, I could flash my demon eyes to clear a path, but these people are old, so they would probably pee their pants or have a heart attack, and that would totally ruin the dining experience.

Glancing back to check once more, I find the waitress has been accosted by an elderly, pink-haired lady. She is speaking very loudly with a strong German accent and gesturing enthusiastically with her hands. She turns, her face creased with wrinkles, and then gives me a quick wink before continuing her loud complaints.

Phew. Thank goodness for the dessert addicted *hausfraus* who understands my plight.

I slow my pace once again and continue to the corner booth I commandeered for my daily dessert dissertation. Luckily, the arrangement of macarons stayed on my plate and didn't drop to the floor in an adult version of Hansel and Gretel.

Placing my plate on the table, I sink down into the booth and examine the mess in front of me. The table is covered in empty plates, and not a single crumb is left on any of them. I'm embarrassed to admit that I may have used my finger to swipe up the rest of a delicious berry coulis that was left on one. Shaking my head, I reach over to the teapot that comes with the high tea buffet deal. It's supposed to be never-ending pots of tea, but the service in this place has left much to be desired, and I find my pot is empty again. I need another pot before I even attempt to eat my macarons.

As I go to signal a waitress, a shadow appears over the table. I look up to find the waitress who was chasing me earlier has finally caught up with me.

"Perfect timing!" I exclaim before she can say anything. "I would love a refill of tea, please. English breakfast. I don't want anything to compete with the flavors of these magnificent macarons." I sigh, looking at them. They are beautiful, shiny, and vibrantly colored, and I'm dying to take a bite.

Her frown deepens before she replies in a condescending tone. "Are you sure you really need to be eating those?" The woman is reed thin and looks like she would snap in a stiff breeze. Her blonde hair is pulled back off her face in a severe bun, and her pursed lips and wrinkled nose make her look like she smelled something rotten.

"Holy fuck!" I exclaim. "What is wrong with your voice?"

High-pitched and nasally, she sounds as bad as nails on a chalkboard.

I start digging around in my bag, pulling out my wallet, phone, and a tampon before grabbing out a throat lozenge I find at the bottom. I offer it to her. "Please, have one. Your customers will kiss my feet."

Her face starts to turn red, and she speaks again, ignoring the offering. "Ma'am, I really think you should probably think twice about eating those macarons."

I look around the room and notice we have an audience, so I talk just a little louder. They shouldn't miss out on the show, and the majority of the patrons look like they are wearing hearing aids.

"Why shouldn't I eat them?" I ask her. "Is this not an all-you-can-eat buffet?"

"Yes, it is, but do you think you need them?" Her eyes run down my body, and her lips sneer in disgust.

"Oh, I see what this is," I announce, standing up to even the playing field. I don't need some skinny bitch trying to lord over me. "Are you implying that my luscious body probably doesn't need any more sweets?" I say, gesturing to it.

A wolf whistle rings out from behind the waitress, and I peer over to see it's the gentleman sitting with my German lifesaver.

I blow him a kiss and return to face Sourpuss McSkinny. "Are you fat-shaming me?"

She shrugs as if to say yes.

"I'd like to speak to your manager, please," I demand and hand her my teapot. "And while you're at it, why don't you take the stick out of your ass and get me some more tea?" I sit back down in the booth and focus on my macarons. Which one should I eat first?

The waitress huffs but does as I requested and disappears. The audience loses interest when nothing happens, turning back to their own delicious desserts. I have tried nearly all the selections on the menu of this new dessert buffet restaurant.

Tasty Treats is a brand-new trending business put together by a culinary school graduate and two others. The menu is extraordinary, and the range of desserts is astronomical. The marketing behind the place is ingenious as well, with monthly theme days for various cultures or countries, weekly senior citizens specials, and mom and baby sessions where they don't allow any other patrons—that way the babies don't disturb the other diners. People flock here in droves. Even now, there is a line of people waiting. It is the perfect place for me to write my new blog piece.

After finally deciding to try the apple pie macaron first, I prepare to take a dainty—yeah right—bite of the delightful greenish red treat, when another shadow falls over the table. The waitress is back, and she brought what could be a sister from another mister with her. Tall, with the same reedy build, blonde, and elegant, she wears a lavender power suit, pearls, and a look of disapproval.

"What seems to be the problem, ma'am?" This one's voice is nasally and unattractive.

"Great Scott!" I exclaim in my best English accent. "Where did the owners employ you from? You all look like you would blow over if someone farted in your direction."

Her nose crinkles up in disgust. The older gentleman who whistled at me earlier outright chuckles, while the other customers all have amused looks on their faces. Of course, they all instantly took notice again as soon as the two women approached me.

"Do any of you even know what the desserts taste like? Or are you all members of the 'eat nothing but air' club?" I know I'm being offensive, but they started it.

When neither responds, I roll my eyes. "I would

like to complain about my treatment. I paid for the all-you-can-eat dessert buffet and never-ending pot of tea, and to be questioned about my consumption by the wait staff is in poor taste."

"Here, here," cheers the German couple, and both women shoot them a dirty look.

The manager turns back to me with a look of disdain, gesturing to the waitress in question. "Well, she does have a point. You've been sitting here for two hours and have just about sampled every item on the buffet. And, well, I'm not sure if you've noticed, but you aren't exactly going to win a Miss America pageant."

I feign a shocked gasp, my hand coming up to my chest as tears well in my eyes. Damn, I'm good. Let's see if she can dig herself any deeper, because out of the corner of my eye, I can see a whole heap of staff who have poked their heads out of the back office and kitchen to watch the showdown.

My voice rises, hitching with emotion. "Are you calling me fat?" Silence surrounds us as the audience waits, and the two women exchange glances.

"If the shoe fits," the waitress says with a shrug.

"If it eats like a pig and waddles like a pig, surely it's a pig," the manager adds.

The restaurant explodes in an uproar. I fake swoon into my booth, and the two women just eye me with contempt.

I close my eyes and pretend to hyperventilate, waving my hands in distress. My breath gets short and choppy, and the room begins to feel warm and suffocating. Crap! I think I took it too far.

Sounds echo in my ears when a hand touches the sleeve of my dress, drawing my attention. The fogginess clears, and I recognize the nasally tone and chalkboard screeching for what it is—two bitches barking out excuses.

Opening my eyes, I see the loveliest sight. It's even more lovely than my plate of macarons, and that's saying something. Crouched down beside me, holding onto my arm, is Mr. Tall, Dark, and Handsome. He must be tall, because even crouched down, his chocolate and caramel eyes are level with mine. His short, stylish hair is dark brown and shot through with streaks of gold and bronze. The well-trimmed scruff on his face matches in color, and my mind immediately wonders what it would feel like against the inside of my thigh. He has a long, slender, aristocratic nose and lips that are succulent and plump. He looks at me with concern, making my heart pound. It's been a long time since my heart got excited about anything but food.

I quickly look at his purlicue to see if he has a demon mark, but he has a hold of my arm from underneath, hiding the webbing between his thumb and first finger. I shake my head when I realize he's talking to me.

Oh, and what a voice. His accent is gently French, like he was born there but hasn't been back in a long time. A little tingle starts in a part of my body not ruled by my stomach.

"I'm sorry, what did you say?" I ask breathlessly. Between my performance and the magnificence of this man, I'm a bit discombobulated.

He smiles gently at me. "I asked if you needed a drink of water."

"I'll have an appletini please."

He blinks, the only sign he's surprised, but smiles as he turns to the waitress.

"Get it," he snaps.

She practically curtsies before scampering away.

He stands up and looks around at the crowd of patrons surrounding us. "Now, can anyone tell me what's actually going on?"

"They called her fat," the old man shouts.

"*Und ein schwein,*" his pink-haired wife chimes in.

"English, woman, English," the old man shouts at his wife, banging his hand on the table.

"Pig. They called her a pig," she amends in heavily accented English.

"Nasty women," they both declare before sitting back down.

The face of the sexy man in front of me becomes thunderous, and he focuses that fury on the manager. "Are they telling the truth, Nicole?" he growls just as the waitress returns with my drink, slamming it down on the table so half of it spills. I study it closely for floating loogies before taking a sip.

Nicole squirms then grows a set of balls and makes a bold move. "Yes, I did. Look at her!" She points her long, boney finger in my direction. "She is… squished into that dress, and her breasts are spilling out everywhere." She turns to me, glaring at me like I am gum on the bottom of her shoe. "You could at least dress for your body type."

"She sampled almost everything on the buffet and kept going back for more," the waitress adds.

The man turns and looks at me. He slowly peruses my body, and a gleam of admiration enters his eyes. I give him a wink and blow him a kiss.

"Stop, you tart!" the manager screeches, obviously losing her control. "Like he would look at a fat cow like you."

Again, the audience gasps in shock, and the man's face turns an alarming shade of red. "This woman is a goddess!" he shouts at her. "All curves and softness. She's someone you wouldn't have to worry about hurting when bending her over a desk." He gives the woman a sneer. "Unlike you."

While absolutely charmed and completely turned on by that declaration, I've finally had enough. All the desserts I consumed are not sitting right with the aggravation in the air. I down the remaining appletini in one go and stand up, smoothing out my long-sleeved, cherry red pin-up dress before grabbing my handbag from the booth. Reaching into my purse, I pull out my business card and hand it to the man. He takes it and glances down before looking back up in surprise. His expression falls when he realizes who I am.

"I'm sorry," I tell them. "You were going to get the Glorious Gluttony seal of approval, a five macaron rating, but I'm afraid your staff leaves much to be desired." I smirk at the women. "And, well, you lost a macaron for each of them. Do yourself a favor and hire some fat women like me. We appreciate food, and we appreciate other people who enjoy food."

The sexy man looks down at my business card in shock. Before he can say anything, I throw two hundred dollars on the table.

"That's for my buffet and the drink," I say, gesturing to the half-assed cocktail, "and for the couple over there." I lift my chin in the older German couple's direction. "Give the change to your bus boy. I'm sure he deserves it more than these two vapid bitches."

With that, I depart with style and grace, waving and blowing kisses to the German couple. I hear shouts of, "Wait!" from behind me, but I ignore them. I have better things to do than get insulted, and no pretty face will change my mind.

Chapter Two

After that disaster, I decide to head home instead of going to the wine bar I was going to review next. My energy is flagging after that unfortunate encounter at Tasty Treats.

I started the Glorious Gluttony food blog as a way to earn my daily energy requirement as a gluttony demon.

That's right. Demons. We are everywhere.

That teacher who yelled a little too much at you in high school? They were probably a wrath demon. That investment banker who gave you great stock advice? That was probably a greed demon. Heck, half of Hollywood's most famous stars are pride or lust demons. We are not much different than humans, except for the three M's—magic, mischief, and mates. Oh, and we are all born in the flames of Hell.

Are we evil? Not any more than humans. It's all about freedom of choice, even for the denizens of Hell.

Demons need to feed on energy to use their powers. If we don't, our energy can get too low and then magic doesn't happen, practically making us human. This is why we work in careers relevant to our specific sin. There are seven different ones, in case you didn't know, which include pride, wrath, sloth, lust, envy, greed, and gluttony.

That's me.

Mom is a lust demon, and Dad is gluttony. I also have two other dads. Papa is a sloth demon, and Father is greed. There are no crossbreeds, so babies will either be one or the other if their parents are different. My twin sister, Serena, is a lust demon, but we both have latent tendencies. She likes food a lot, and I like men, also a lot. Serena isn't fussy and goes both ways, but I am partial to thick, rock-hard… bodies.

My much younger brothers are sloth and greed respectively, like their dads. Yep, lots of dads. Lust demons and demons with lust tendencies tend to have multiple partners. Fated mates make it easy for lust demons, but until they find their mates, they need other ways to feed. Serena owns an escort service and charges an arm and a leg for sex, and she gets well fed in the process. No judgment here. Lucky bitch.

Demons are identified by a small symbol that appears on their purlicue, which is the little bit of skin between the thumb and first finger. At the onset of puberty, a symbol appears that designates our class of demon. The gluttony mark is a little circle with the symbol for pi in it with two boobs on either end of the horizontal line. They are black when they first appear, and we know when we have met our mates after one touch of their skin because the symbol changes color. For gluttony, it's orange. We also get a ring of our mate's sin color around our symbol.

Entering the apartment I share with my sister, I throw my keys in the bowl on the little table in the hallway near the front door. I glance down at my hand and notice my symbol is still black. Well, I guess it was just wishful thinking on my part. I couldn't even see if he was a demon, plus he didn't touch my skin. Damn, the man was smoking hot.

I hear music playing in the kitchen, and the smell of food drifts down the hallway, lighting my tummy on fire again. I head in that direction, of course, and find my sister dancing and singing into a wooden spoon as she works. She hasn't noticed me yet, so I lean against the doorframe, smiling in amusement. Although we're twins, we are opposites. I'm tall and she's short. Both of us are curvy in all the right places, but I have to work hard not to lean toward chunky. She has ice-blonde, curly hair, whereas mine is a dark, mahogany brown and dead straight. We both have plump, full lips and arched eyebrows, but my eyes are light blue and hers are a pretty pale green.

Her ass wiggles as she bops in time to some K-pop rubbish, stirring something in a frying pan on the stove. She puts in a Michael Jackson worthy screech and spins, noticing me standing there.

"Hey, bitch," she says, waving her spoon at me. "Food's almost done. Grab us some wine, will you?"

I push off the doorframe and open the fridge to inspect the wine options. Grabbing a bottle of white, I get two glasses from the cupboard above the counter and pour.

"You're… energetic. Have a good day?" I ask after taking a sip of my wine. The sharp, fruity flavors burst across my tongue before the cool liquid slides down my throat. Sitting down at the kitchen bench, I feel the last bit of tension leave my body.

Serena dishes the food onto plates and passes me one before sitting down next to me. "God, yes. My client today was so enthusiastic, I feel like I'll have energy for days. Four orgasms in the space of an hour. He really knew what he was doing." She sighs. "Why can't I find one like that in real life?"

"Demon or human?" I ask, taking a bite of my food.

"Who? Oh, the client. Lust demon. Humans just don't cut it compared to demons. They work in a pinch, but demons give off way more energy when fucking." She blows out a breath. "Some lust demons prefer to pay for it, with the amount of sex they need to keep full. There's no point in leading on willing partners when you know you have a mate somewhere. Those ones are the keepers. They are responsible, honest, and trustworthy."

She hunches her shoulders, and a note of sadness colors her voice. "Why can't I just find a mate or two? I'm not greedy. I just want a steady, consistent source of energy, and I want to cuddle, damn it!"

I laugh at that. "What am I, chopped liver?"

She frowns at me. "You don't put out."

We both crack up laughing. I shovel more food into my mouth, faster than normal, but my energy is low after the drama at the restaurant. Serena eyes the way I scarf down the food, and I can see the questions in her eyes.

"Why are you so hungry? I thought you were reviewing Tasty Treats today. All-you-can-eat desserts. You should be in foodie nirvana!"

"I'm not sure, actually. I did eat well, but then these skinny bitches gave me a hard time. I gave it right back, and the owner got involved. By the time I got home, all the good energy was gone." My heart rate picks up at the thought of the gorgeous French guy.

No, Glory! No point crying over spilled milk.

Milk. Maybe we have some ice cream. I get up from the bench and open the freezer. Pulling out a tub of Ben and Jerry's Bob Marley One Love ice cream, I grab a spoon and sit back down.

Serena continues to watch me with raised eyebrows. "Maybe I should set you up with my guy from today. Even if he's not your mate, he has a big cock and knows how to use it."

"You know I'm not completely hopeless," I mumble around a mouthful of ice cream. "I bet the guy I met today had a big cock, and I bet he knows how to use it too. Maybe I'll go back next week and try the buffet again, see if I can catch the staff's attention." I shrug and continue to eat my ice cream, not caring about much else.

I watch as she puts our plates in the dishwasher, then grabs the laptop and brings it back to the bench. She opens it up and starts tapping at the keys, her long, pointy nails making it a slow process.

I'm too enthralled with the banana, caramelly goodness to ask what she's doing.

"I know what will cheer you up. Look!" Serena says, pointing to the screen. "Kelly, the wedding coordinator at the manor, has sent us a notice about a wedding tomorrow, with a full, premium smorgasbord. Apparently, the wedding is huge, and two extra guests wouldn't be noticed. There's also no seating plan, so we won't have to worry about finding a space left by no-shows."

I just shrug again before digging for more ice cream, only to realize the tub's empty. Tears start to form in my eyes.

Serena gets a worried look on her face and then goes into crisis mode. She runs to the pantry and pulls out a box of gourmet chocolates and flings them in my direction. They slide across the bench and land in front of me. I turn my nose up.

Gaping at me in shock, she runs to the freezer

and pulls out another tub of ice cream, this time B and J's plain vanilla, and tosses that in my direction. She starts pulling out syrups, cream, nuts, and sprinkles then goes to the nearby fruit bowl and grabs a banana, which she peels quickly before putting it in a sundae glass and placing it in front of me. By the time she's finished, there's a panicked glint in her eye.

"Eat, Glory, eat. The last time you were so emotional, you went on a five-week bender that emptied the city of its pancake supply. We're still banned from all the IHOPs in the state." She cuts the banana in half, spoons ice cream on top, and adds all the available sundae trimmings. Once done, she moves the chocolate box out of the way and replaces it with a sundae almost as big as my head.

Overcome with gratitude, I just nod in her direction and dig in.

She nudges me in the side and continues to ramble. "Come on. We'll go to the wedding, eat lots of delicious food, and maybe pick up a couple of single men. You know a wedding is a surefire place to get laid, what with all the single people who are feeling desperate."

I shoot her a crabby look and growl a little.

"Not that I'm saying we can only get laid if someone is desperate," she says, backpedaling. "We're hot. They would be lucky."

I nod and continue to eat. I hear a breath escape her mouth before she continues.

"By the end of the night, both our appetites will be sated. We'll be happy little demons, Glory."

I contemplate the idea.

"And you know what?" She has a twinkle in her eye again, and a mischievous grin crosses her face. "We can plan revenge against Tasty Treats. They must pay for treating you like this, and I'm not just talking about bad reviews."

I'm starting to feel better after all the calories I've consumed, and revenge is starting to sound good. Sugar is running through my system, and my energy is increasing exponentially.

"You know what?" I begin, waving my spoon around. "The best revenge I could get against those skinny bitches would be to get that gorgeous hunk of a man to bend me over one of the tables." I jump out of my seat, her idea growing on me by the second. "I'm in. The manor's premium smorgasbord is one of my favorites. Casual sex for dessert, and then plan revenge. What a well-rounded meal."

Serena slumps in relief.

"What's your problem?" I ask her.

"You're not you when you're hungry." She snaps her fingers, and a Snickers bar appears in her hand.

I blink before bursting out laughing and pull her against me in a one-armed hug. "I'm sorry, Reni," I tell her. "Today was a clusterfuck. I'm so lucky to have you looking after me." I kiss her head. "I think I'll head upstairs. I need to post my scathing review of Tasty Treats." I wrinkle my nose in disappointment. "The desserts tasted like they were made by angels. Seriously, I want to find the chef and have his babies." I head to my bedroom but pause, putting my hand on the doorframe. "Hey, do you think the beautiful man was the chef? Damn it, why didn't I ask?" I kick the doorframe in frustration. "Fucking skinny bitches, messing with my game. They will pay."

Serena is staring at me in horror again, and I look down. My body is on fire, and the doorframe I'm clutching starts to smolder, although my clothes seem to be intact and my body only feels slightly warm.

"Oops. Fuck!" I shout. I take a few deep breaths to calm myself, and the flames finally go out. Serena grabs a tea towel and starts smacking the doorframe with it until it stops smoking.

"Well, that was new," Serena comments sarcastically, throwing the tea towel in the trash. "I'm going to call Mom and the dads and see if they know what that was about. Try to stay calm until we figure it out. Go roll a joint, and for goodness' sake, don't burn our house down."

I throw a one-fingered salute in her direction and head for my bedroom, muttering, "Not like I did it on purpose, bitch."

I manage to type out my review without setting the room on fire or melting the laptop in the process. Once I finish, I head to bed, not bothering with any of my usual pre-bedtime routine. I just can't bring myself to care. My energy has disappeared again. What is going on? In the past, a meal like the one I had today would sustain me for an entire day, sometimes two.

I spend the night tossing and turning in my bed, annoyed that those skinny bitches and their reactions are still bothering me. The scene repeats in my head like an endless loop, their faces appearing in my dreams, telling me I'm too fat to get a man like him. The man in question then shakes his head and tells me I'm beautiful and kisses me like I'm his world, but they tear us apart.

I'm lying on the buffet table surrounded by cakes and desserts and a bowl of juicy red apples. A little black and white snake slithers around them, its tongue flickering in and out. I look down, and I'm naked. The beautiful man has his head between my legs, devouring me like I did the buffet. Just as I'm about to orgasm, he is ripped away. I try to sit up, but my hands are trapped in bowls of jelly. I'm surrounded by donuts, macarons, cakes, and cookies, and I can't reach any of them. I look up, and that uppity manager is leaning over me. I struggle but can't escape as she grabs a cake knife and slams it into my chest. My mouth is wide open as if to scream in terror when the snake slithers in. I start to choke before suddenly bolting upright in bed.

My heart beats as fast as a hummingbird's wings, and tears stream down my face. I look around. Was that a shadow at my window? No, nothing but the moonlight streams through. I must have forgotten to close the curtains before I went to bed. My breathing slows, as does my heart rate.

Getting up, I go to my attached bathroom to get myself a drink of water. On the way back, I pull the curtains closed and quickly jump into bed, pulling up my covers. That dream was really good until the end. Being denied an orgasm then stabbed in the chest? Man, that was mean.

***

*B*efore the wedding, I decide I need some extra pampering. I'm feeling rough and low on energy, which I can't seem to maintain. Sleep never did come easily to me after that bad dream woke me.

The bathwater bubbles and fizzes with the bath bomb I throw in, and the room fills with the scent of jasmine and oranges as the water turns a light yellow color. I put my hair up in a messy bun and climb into the bath. The warm water cocoons my body, and my muscles relax one by one. Closing my eyes, I clear my mind of any thoughts and just float.

Finally, the water cools off too much and I decide to get out. Wrapping myself in a fluffy pink towel, I survey my wardrobe options. I'm not fat, but I do have curves in all the right places. Think Marilyn Monroe—gorgeous and curvy, though overweight by today's standards, which is ridiculous.

I pull out a cute little cocktail dress. The bodice is made from eggplant-colored lace, with capped sleeves and a plunging neckline. Strategically placed lace flowers cover my nipples. The royal purple satin skirt flares out at my hips in a tutu style, with several layers of tulle, and a bright purple ribbon wraps around my waist. I pull on the dress and twirl in front of the mirror. It sits beautifully, accentuating my breasts and waistline. I grab a pair of black suede platform heels with satin ribbons that wrap up around my calves.

Moving on to hair and makeup, I opt for a tousled, sexy bedhead look with soft curls, a purple smoky eye, and a deep maroon lipstick. After grabbing a black wrap and clutch, I head out to see if Serena is ready. When I get to the kitchen, I find her sipping a glass of wine, ready to go.

She, too, is wearing all lace. Her dress is a pale green number that hugs her body in all the right places, finishing at mid-thigh, and her normally curly hair has been straightened and looks very sleek. She looks amazing.

After giving me the once-over, she nods her head. "If that doesn't get you laid, nothing will." Finishing her wine, she goes to the cupboard and pulls out a box of donuts. "Here, this should keep you going until we get to the reception. Thank goodness we don't have to sit through a long ceremony."

I look at the donuts unenthusiastically, screwing up my nose.

Her mouth drops open. "What is wrong with you?" she asks, placing her hand on my forehead to check my temperature.

I swat her away. "I don't know. I had all these weird dreams, I caught on fire, and I can't seem to maintain my energy. Not only that, but I also don't want those doughnuts," I wail, holding back my tears, not wanting to smudge my makeup. "Did you speak to Mom or our dads?"

She shakes her head. "No. I tried, but no one is answering. I'll try again." She pulls out her phone, but I hold up my hand.

"We don't have time. We have to go, or we'll be too late, and we won't be able to blend in with the guests."

She puts the phone back in her clutch. "Okay, but if something else weird happens, I'll call them immediately."

When we get to the manor, our friend Kelly meets us in the foyer and leads us to a large area outside. She's a pride demon, and as a wedding coordinator, she feeds off the pride of brides and grooms when their weddings go exactly like they planned.

"Girls, you all look gorgeous with a capital G, but Glory, you're looking a little pale." She frowns at me. "Are you okay?" she asks, her southern accent getting stronger with her concern.

"Just ready to get my eats on, Kelly." I shoot for a brilliant smile, but I'm afraid it leaves a lot to be desired, because both Kelly and Serena are watching me very carefully.

Kelly directs us behind a large tree and peeks around it to make sure no one is looking. The area has a huge wisteria arbor covering it, the sweet smell of the flowers drifting on the gentle breeze. Tables and chairs are placed around a dance floor, and a long buffet table is on the opposite side of where we stand.

"Appetizers are being offered, so have a few of those to start with. The buffet will start when the bride and groom arrive," Kelly explains. "They didn't want their guests to have to wait for speeches before they eat, so they'll be done during the meal. They don't care if people get up and move around while they are talking. The singles selection today is out of this world," she says, turning to Serena, "but for goodness' sake, if you're going to fuck them in the bathroom, lock the door!"

I laugh at that comment, and Serena turns a pretty shade of pink. She's not normally easy to embarrass, but when you get caught giving oral sex to the bride because you forgot to lock the door? Yeah, the commotion that resulted was memorable, especially since she was caught by the bride's grandmother. Serena used her power to fade into invisibility, literally, that day.

"Have fun, ladies, and feed well," Kelly says as she gives us both a kiss on the cheek. "If you get caught, I will deny knowing you." With that, she disappears into the crowd of arriving guests.

Waiters start to circle by with trays of appetizers and glasses of champagne. Smoothing down my dress, I turn to Serena.

"Okay, what are we going with today?" I ask her, knowing she would have done her research last night.

"We are Great-Aunt Leigh's granddaughters on the groom's side. His family is huge, and a couple of extras won't be noticed, unlike the bride who only has her brother and not many friends."

With a nod, we leave our hiding place and seamlessly blend in. I grab two glasses of champagne off a tray and hand one to Serena, tracking an appetizer platter like I'm a heat-seeking missile and it's a ball of flames. Indelicately, I take a couple of pieces of whatever it is, possibly crab cakes, but at this stage, I'm really not fussy. Serena tracked another one down and is loading up a napkin to bring back to me. I move to the side and start shoveling food into my mouth.

Serena does a great job of bringing me more treats, and I just continue to eat, but I move around a few times so as not to attract attention. Feeling slightly more like myself, I finish off my glass of champagne and begin to pay attention to my surroundings. Serena joins me, and we start to scope out potential partners for her to get a little action.

"What about that one?" I ask, pointing to a good-looking gentleman, but before she can look, he lifts his left hand, and I see the glint of a wedding ring. "Never mind," I mutter.

I keep looking, but a commotion over at the entrance to the garden draws our attention. We turn to see the bridal party entering the reception, followed by the bride and groom, who appear to be genuinely in love.

Serena doesn't touch the ones who are in love, and yes, we demons can just tell. Occasionally, Serena will try to score with either the bride or groom, but only the ones who aren't going to make it. It's a challenge to her, and the thrill gives her a bigger feed.

We move on to the rest of the bridal party. There are four groomsmen, all dressed in smart black suits with gray ties. I can't see any of their faces, though they all look tall, and two have dark hair while the other two have lighter locks. I move on to the bridesmaids. They are all wearing elegant, fitted dresses with scoop neck backs, all in the same gray as the groomsmen. They smile as they make their way to the bridal table.

To my horror, I recognize two of the bridesmaids, and it's like cartoon sirens start wailing in my head with big, flashing lights.

"Fuck," I say entirely too loudly. I duck behind a rather large man who's standing in front of me.

Serena looks at me in concern again. Poor Serena. I'm going to give her an ulcer. Well, I would if demons could get them.

She raises an eyebrow in question.

"The skinny bitches are in the bridal party, the two blondes on the end," I whisper.

She looks at them and nods.

"They are the ones from yesterday."

She gets a glint in her eye and starts to head toward them, so I grab her hand and yank her back.

"Don't blow our cover," I hiss. "I need to eat, damn it. I'll just avoid them."

This time, she gasps out loud, and now it's my turn to look at her with concern.

"What?"

"Mr. Big Cock and Knows How to Use It is here."

"Huh?" I'm confused.

"My demon client from yesterday is one of the groomsmen."

I angle my head around the body of the man I'm using for cover, but before I can see whom she's referring to, my stomach clenches as I recognize yet another person. My head drops in utter disbelief.

"Abort, abort!" I hiss, grabbing Serena and dragging her toward an exit.

She pulls me to a stop. "Damn it, Glory! What are you doing?"

"The beautiful man from yesterday is here too. He's in the bridal party! It's a clusterfuck." I shake free of her grip and keep walking. "Let's just go and crash a Bar Mitzvah or... hey, I hear church potlucks are a thing."

I stay hidden behind people and keep my head down, focusing on the exit. I'm ducking and weaving through the crowd like a dancer on crack when screeching feedback from a speaker rings out across the area. Everyone stops what they are doing and pauses to listen to the MC. I stop too. If I continue the way I'm going, it will be too noticeable.

I sit down at a free table. Serena catches up and collapses in a chair next to me, shooting me an evil look as she waits for the MC to give out information. The buffet is being served. It looks like an army of ants is scurrying out of the building toward the long table, where they place their offerings before scurrying back.

The bride stands up and takes the microphone, her sweet voice ringing out over the reception as she gestures to the buffet table. "Join us for our first meal as a married couple!"

Shouts of joy ring out from the crowd, followed by a thunderous applause. I stand up to continue my escape, but Serena tugs me back down.

"What. Are. You. Doing?" I hiss, punctuating each word.

"We're here now, and we're even at a table, so let's just eat and socialize a bit. We know to avoid the bridal table, but we do that at most weddings we crash," she says a little too loudly.

The other occupants at the table shoot her suspicious looks, but they are distracted by people getting up to go to the buffet, and they soon join the line.

Serena and I know the deal. We avoid the first rush, which will include the bridal party, and wait calmly for the next round of food to be brought out. That round will be fresh off the stove too, not sitting in warmers for who knows how long. I reluctantly agree to stay, so we both snag another glass of champagne off the tray and wait our turn.

Besides, what are the odds that I'll run into the bitches in this crowd of three hundred?

Chapter Four

"God," I groan, rubbing my belly. "I feel so much better. I really needed that." I've been to the buffet twice, and Serena has been for me too. Thankfully, it isn't too close to the bridal table, so we've been able to avoid the skinny bitches.

She stops talking to the couple on her other side and looks at me closely. "You look way better too. You have some color back in your skin and a sparkle in your eye."

I give her a smile. "Okay, Serena. It's scoping out time. We need to find you someone to bang." I sit up in my seat and survey the area. The guests have mostly finished eating. A few stragglers are heading back and forth, but it looks like the staff is breaking down the buffet to set up the desserts. People have started moving around and mingling, which makes checking out the talent easier.

Just as I'm about to point someone out to Serena, I spot something that makes my heart skip a beat. The manager of Tasty Treats is heading in our direction. She hasn't noticed me yet, so I quickly dive under the table. The grass tickles my knees as I curl into a ball. Luckily, there's only us and one other couple sitting here, so there's plenty of room for me underneath.

"What are you doing, Glory? For fuck's sake, are you going insane?" Serena rants. "Your behavior is ridiculous. I'm calling Mom." My sister peers at me under the table.

I wave her away. "Skinny bitch is heading our way. Stop looking at me."

Serena puts a small smile on her face and sits up.

"Charles, Diana, how are you?" I hear that nasally voice ask the other couple at our table.

"Wow, that's one hell of a voice. How does anyone listen to that?" Serena asks her.

Fuck, she's going to blow our cover.

"Who are you?" Nicole demands. "I don't know you, and I know everyone." I can just picture her snooty nose in the air as she looks down at Serena with disdain. "Never mind, I don't care. You can't be important, or I would know you. Anyway, I was just looking for the children from the bridal party. They want a photo around the cake. Have you seen them?"

I hear Diana and Charles reply in the negative, and then I hear a deep voice chime in.

"Have you checked under the tables?"

Oh, that voice with that beautiful, gentle French accent.

Wait, what did he say? Fuck! I throw myself

onto my hands and knees and start rapidly crawling away in the opposite direction of where they are located.

With stealthy, ninja-like skills, I furiously crawl to the next table, but I don't stop. I want to put some space between me and the table I just left. Let's face it, if they look under one, there's a good chance they'll look under them all, so I keep going.

Pausing briefly to catch my breath, I look down at my knees and see they have a light green tinge to them now. I peer out to survey the situation. The staff has placed a small table near the bridal table, which holds a magnificent wedding cake.

There are no signs of the children yet. Crap, I need to keep moving. I can still hear that nasally voice, but I think she's still a couple of tables behind me. I scurry to the next table quickly and come to an abrupt stop.

"Shit."

The table is already occupied. A sea of gray taffeta and tulle is ensconced under the table, encapsulating a trio of giggling girls. Two girls look to be about five years old. One is blonde-haired and blue-eyed, and the other is black-haired with piercing green eyes. The last little girl is about three, also with black hair and green eyes. Sisters? Each has chocolate smeared across their face, and they all look to be very pleased with themselves.

"You said shit," the blonde accuses, pointing at me.

"Yep." I drag myself farther under the table. It's crowded, and I'm now pushed up against someone's legs. Hopefully they think I'm a child. I shift awkwardly so I'm sitting cross-legged.

"But you know what?" I ask the girls. "There's a woman who's looking for you three, and I was trying to stay in front of her. I was not expecting to find you." Worried looks cross their faces.

"Does she have blonde hair and a voice that sounds like she has a blocked nose?" the older, dark-haired girl asks, pointing at her own.

I nod my head, and a look of fear crosses their faces. They scramble into motion but stop abruptly when that nasally voice calls just above our heads. This is my cue to scramble into action, but I forget that I'm trapped by a pair of legs, and I end up launching myself face-first into somebody's crotch.

Oh my god, could things get any worse? I'm about to be discovered by that witch, and now I am motorboating a strange man's penis. Yes, I know it's a penis because it just jumped under my face. The person who owns the lap moves his chair back slightly and peers under the table.

"Nolan, have you seen your girls?" the nasally bitch asks. "We need all of you for a photo by the wedding cake." She pauses. "What are you looking at under the table? Is it them?"

I look back, and the girls are all staring at the man, shaking their heads. I join in. The man has piercing green eyes that are eerily similar to the girls', and he has a stunned look on his face. I guess that's not surprising, considering I introduced my face to his penis.

The girls are imploring him with their little hands clasped in prayer, so I do the same and beg with my eyes. His gaze goes from them to me. Seeing me at his feet, begging, must be appealing to him, because heat fills his eyes before he lowers the tablecloth.

My head drops to my chest in relief. Oh. Well, it might be my tits that appealed to him too. With all the crawling, my dress is pulled down to just above my nipples, and I have cleavage you could park a bike in.

I straighten myself out, and the girls and I wait with bated breath to see what he does.

"No, Nicole, I haven't seen them." His voice sends a shiver straight down my spine. Growly and deep, it does all sorts of things to my body. "I thought I dropped my napkin under the table."

All four of us let out a quiet sigh of relief.

"Why don't you check at the front of the house? The girls like to watch the koi fish in the pond," he continues. "I think they saved a bread roll to feed the fish."

The smallest girl lifts a bread roll to show me, and we exchange a grin.

Nicole, nasally bitch, makes a sound. "Eww, really?" Her tone causes us to wince. "Fine." She sighs in exasperation.

Smiles of joy and relief cover the girls' faces.

After a moment, the man says, "Alright, she's gone. Out you come."

The girls scramble out from under the table, but I stay put, hoping he'd forgotten about me.

"You too, princess."

Damn it. My heart starts to beat a little faster as I, too, crawl out, stand up, and smooth out my dress. I look up into the eyes of the man in front of us and feel like I'm being scolded as well.

"Why were you hiding from Nicole?" he asks the girls. "She's looking all over for you. It's for Aunty Bella."

"Not another photo, Daddy," the youngest one pleads, tugging on his pant leg. The other two are shaking their heads.

"She's so mean," the blonde-haired girl chimes in. "She pinches us if we don't move fast enough."

He looks at her in surprise, and they all nod their heads.

"Why did Aunty Bella ask her to be in the wedding, Daddy?" the oldest asks.

"Because of Louis. Damn fool," he mutters under his breath. "And what's your excuse?" he asks, looking at me.

"She's mean, and she pinches," I reply solemnly, sending the girls into fits of giggles.

He raises his eyebrows at me. "Really?"

I nod my head.

He sighs, exasperated. "Okay, you rug rats, get

out of here. I'll tell Aunty Bella that you've had enough. She'll be cranky, but she'll get over it, I hope. God help me." He sends up a prayer for help.

The girls wave to me and run off, so I turn and try to make my escape.

"Not you!" That voice hits me in just the right spot, and my latent lust demon pokes her head up.

"Now, I don't recognize you, and I thought I knew everyone my sister invited," the gruff voice says.

I turn slowly, my heartbeat increasing, and then look around for Serena in the hopes that she'll swoop in and save me. I can see the bitch watching from the table with an amused look on her face. That bitch will pay! I plaster on a smile and face him fully.

"Hi! I'm Great-Aunt Leigh's granddaughter, Glory." I can see he doesn't believe me.

"Great-Aunt Leigh is a raging dyke and never had any children," he deadpans.

My heart drops. Fucking Serena.

He points out a gorgeous older woman on the other side of the reception. She has gray-streaked auburn hair that's pulled back in a tight updo and is wearing a pantsuit that fits beautifully on her tall, slender frame. A long string of pearls hangs around her neck, and she has a pair of tortoiseshell glasses perched on her nose. I watch as she drags deeply on a cigarette, and when she blows out the smoke, I can hear her husky bellow of laughter.

Okay! Time to make a getaway.

I spin quickly, taking a couple of steps, but before I can get far, I feel a hand on my arm. Suddenly, I'm spun around, and the guy looks furious. Before I can say anything, I feel a sharp pain in my hand, like I've been stung by a wasp. I look down, and my demon mark has changed color. It's now bright orange. A feeling of joy flows through my body, and when I look up, the man seems just as stunned as I am. He's also looking at his hand in shock. In fact, he looks like he could be knocked over with a feather.

"Mate?" he rasps.

I nod hopefully. He looks faint and sits down on his chair again.

What's with the reaction? I look down at myself. I'm not that horrific, am I? I mean, I know I have a few more curves than a lot of the women here, but I'm not huge. Discreetly, I drop my nose down to my armpits and sniff. Nope, I smell fine. Now I'm starting to get annoyed. I put my hands on my hips, ready to ask what his problem is, when two little angels run back to us.

"Daddy." They wrap their arms around him, and my heart drops.

I sink down onto a seat, my joy at finding my mate shattering when I realize he must already have one. I'm going to be a sister-wife. The man who's supposed to be my soulmate already has children with another—two beautiful little girls who look just like their daddy, unless their mom has the same coloring.

My womb weeps. They should be my children. I know I'm being ridiculous, since many demons have multiple mates. I mean, I have three dads. I just didn't expect to be the one who had to share. A tear escapes the corner of my eye before I can control it.

"Daddy, Aunty Bella is looking for you. She's angry." This seems to shock him out of his stupor. He looks at the girls and then at me. Over his shoulder, I see the bride storming toward us. She's a woman on a mission, and she looks pissed.

He shifts his gaze between us. "My sister is a wrath demon. I really need to see what's wrong, or shit could hit the fan."

I look down at his hand. His mark is a circle with a smaller circle inside, with three even smaller circles spread evenly around it—red. He's a wrath demon. I take a step backward.

"Please wait," he begs, holding up his hands.

Shaking my head, I turn and flee.

Chapter Five

I hear shouting behind me, but I ignore it. I run awkwardly past Serena, my heels making it difficult to gain any kind of speed on the grass. She has a worried look on her face, but again, I ignore it and keep going.

I leave the reception area, and I'm about to round the corner of the manor when I run face-first into a brick wall—a brick wall that screeches as we both tumble to the ground. Arms flailing and legs tangled, I recognize those nasally tones. Abuse flies out of that mouth, but I tune it all out. Rolling onto my back, I drop my head onto the ground and look up at the sky. White clouds drift slowly above me, fluffy and insubstantial, much like my energy. Once again, it has completely dissipated. Nothing is left. Zip. Nada. Zippo. Bupkis. Just like that, I feel like I have hit rock bottom.

Movement around me jolts me out of my musings. Slowly, my ears tune back into the conversation.

"What are you doing here? Are you crashing the wedding? You weren't on the guest list!"

I turn my head to the side and see Nicole giving me a glare that could freeze Hell. Lethargy has taken over my body, and I ignore her. Getting up, I straighten my dress out again and continue in the direction I was going, but she doesn't give up. She grabs my arm, and that is the last straw.

I turn, snarling in her direction, my body once again bursting into flames. "Get your fucking hands off me."

She yanks her hand back, squealing in pain. Rubbing it against her dress, she backs away and places her hands on her hips. "I asked you what you're doing here, fatty."

The flames surrounding my body rise higher at the insult. I feel like I could set the whole world ablaze and watch it burn, not caring one little bit. Serena has caught up to me now, and I see the bride and her brother just behind her. In fact, we have attracted quite a bit of attention. Serena tries to talk me down.

"Deep breaths, Glory. Think happy thoughts. Cake, chocolate, macarons." The flames die down a little, and the two little girls who have followed their aunt and father join in on the suggestions.

"Rainbow, unicorns, fluffy bunnies!" the older one says.

"Money!" the little one shouts, causing the surrounding people to laugh, and the flames sputter away, but then she yells out, "Daddy!" and the flames flare again, this time shooting outwards.

Luckily no one is hurt, except I can see Nicole's hair smoldering. I'm not going to tell her. Hopefully by the time she smells it, it will be a roaring forest fire in that hairdo that's been hair sprayed to death.

"It's not going to work," I hear the bride, Bella, tell Serena. "That's mate fire. I had the same problem. Until she fu—" She stops abruptly, looking at the girls. "Seals her bond, she'll keep bursting into flames, and her energy will be practically nonexistent. When I met Felix, every tiny little thing set off my anger. I almost burned the house down, and even though I own a call center and was continuously bombarded by people's wrath, I was starving."

"That's what that is?" Serena looks incredulously between Bella and me. "I don't think Mom ever mentioned it before."

Bella shakes her head. "It's rare, and not all demons experience it. Her mate should be able to calm her down with his touch."

Serena looks back at me again. Although I'm on fire, a tear drips down my face, impervious to the flames. "Oh, honey, what's wrong?" she asks. "You should be over the moon. Who is it?"

Bella and I both turn to look at her brother. Serena looks between Bella's brother and me, and then to the children behind him. I see the exact moment when she realizes what's happened. She turns back to me.

"Baby girl, I'm sorry." Serena instinctively

knows how I'm feeling—it's a twin thing. The joy is replaced with heartbreak when she realizes he must already have a partner and that he has children from another woman.

A shrieking sound pierces our little bubble, and we watch as Nicole dances around, trying to put out her smoking hair. Skinny bitch number one has joined us, and she runs to a nearby table, grabs a pitcher of water, and flings it at Nicole. Water and ice fly through the air. Another shriek sounds out, and although her hair is no longer on fire, she is dripping wet with mascara running down her face.

"Fuck, I hope you had all your photos done," I mutter, making the offhanded comment to Bella. For a moment, I think she's going to blow her top, but then she bursts out laughing instead.

"Oh my god, that is awesome. I can't stand those women! They are only in the party because they were dating Felix's best friend and brother. Unfortunately, when they broke up with them, it was too late to change."

"Stop laughing, just stop it. Mate fire? What poor person is mated to this fat cow?" Nicole spits, but her mouth drops open when Bella's brother takes a step toward me.

"Nolan, you can't seriously be mated to this fatty-bom-bah," the other skinny bitch sneers.

My flames flicker like an out of control wildfire. He steps closer, and I take another step back. Bella watches us shrewdly as my eyes dart between Nolan and the girls, and then she steps in.

"Glory?" She shoots me a sad smile as I nod my head. "Just let him stop the fire for you, then we can all sit down and talk about everything. It will work itself out. We can get you some more food. Having him sit next to you will go a long way in helping you even out your emotions."

Serena nods her head in encouragement, and while they both distract me, Nolan sneaks up, reaching through my fire and grabbing my hands. I look down in amazement as he gently squeezes my fingers, and then back up into his piercing green eyes. He's smiling.

"Tickles. It feels good," he says, the stress lines easing from his face. We both stand there staring at each other. My flames bathe us in warmth before slowly dying down and then sputtering out completely.

I quickly drop his hands, and Serena throws her arms around me, pushing him out of the way.

"Your mate is hot," she whispers in my ear.

I look over her shoulder and give him a good once-over. Broad shoulders taper down into a slender waist, and his white button-up shirt is sinfully tight, showcasing his amazing body to the fullest. His black hair is styled in a sexy way that looks like it needs a cut but is actually styled to perfection, and it has a bit of gray scattered at the temples. Nolan has plump lips surrounded by well-groomed facial hair, waiting for me to take a bite. The man is fine.

He looks down, and I follow his gaze. His little girls have wrapped their arms around his legs and are watching everything intensely. The older one is giving me a fierce look, and the younger one has her thumb in her mouth.

Serena lets go of me and turns back around to Bella and Nolan. She can tell that I'm still in shock, so she takes over.

"I'm Serena, and this is my sister, Glory. I'm sorry we were crashing your wedding. It's what we do." She shrugs her shoulders unapologetically. "But usually, no one even notices."

I snort in disgust. "Yet this one has been one clusterfu—fudge after another."

Bella insists on hearing the tale, so instead of making our escape, we find ourselves once again seated at a table, this time surrounded by people intent on listening to the story.

Nolan tells the girls to go feed the koi in the front pond, so they run off to find their friend Ella. That's a good thing, because this story isn't for little ears.

Bella's new husband, Felix, has also joined us, while B1 and B2, aka Nicole and Jenny, demand to hear the story. They have smug looks on their faces, probably hoping Bella's wrath demon is going to come out to play, but by now, I don't care. We are also joined by Bella's best friend Lizzie, young Ella's mother.

Bella has some food brought over while Serena starts the story. Before the story begins, though, two gentlemen join us at the table. Bella refers to them as Felix's brother and best friend. The thunk of my head hitting the table is loud enough to make people jump. Luckily, I miss my plate of food.

Seriously, what is bigger than a clusterfuck? Because that's what this is. The first gentleman is the beautiful man from the restaurant yesterday, and judging by the look on Serena's face, the second is her client with a big cock.

I start to laugh hysterically, tears streaming down my face. Serena's mouth is open in shock, then she looks at me and joins in. We are both in tears, clutching each other, while the table's occupants look at us like we have lost our minds.

We calm down, and I wipe my eyes with a napkin. Serena takes a sip of water from a glass and sets it back on the table before beginning the story.

"Glory had a bad day yesterday. It seems that the restaurant she was reviewing for her blog needs to reassess its management and wait staff."

"You were the blogger at Tasty Treats yesterday?" Nolan asks abruptly.

I nod my head in surprise.

"I am so sorry for your treatment," he grovels.

"We had no idea they spoke to the customers like that. Apparently, you're not the first. The other staff informed us of their behavior. That problem has been rectified."

I raise my eyebrows and turn to look at B1 and B2. They are rolling their eyes.

Jenny shoots me a hateful glare. "You got us fired, bitch."

Serena's client shakes his head.

"No, you did that to yourselves, you vapid cow. I heard about your treatment of paying customers. Why are they even here?" he asks Bella and Felix with an exasperated look. "We broke up with them for a reason."

Bella growls, and her eyes flash red. "They are only here because you and Louis have shitty taste, and when you broke up with them, it was too late to change the wedding plans." Felix rubs her back and whispers in her ear. The red fades from her eyes, and she takes a deep breath.

"What does that have to do with either of you?" Serena asks, gesturing to Nolan and her client, whose real name I still don't know.

I don't suppose I can call him Mr. Big Cock and Knows How to Use It, huh?

Mr. Beautiful, who I now know is Louis, steps up. "Nolan and Carter are the other owners of Tasty Treats," he informs me. His French accent sends tingles across my skin. "I tried to get you to stop yesterday, but I don't think you heard me."

I roll my eyes. "Oh, I heard you, I just didn't care," I sneer at him, not ready to forgive my treatment at the hands of those petty bitches.

"Anyway," Bella interrupts, gesturing toward Serena. "Go on with the story."

"Saturdays are our wedding crashing days," Serena continues. "I was feeling full of energy after a very satisfying romp yesterday." She gives her client, who I now know is Carter, a wink. "I hated seeing her so low, so I planned this wedding crash. We do it regularly to scope out easy singles for me and fabulous food for her. It satisfies both our demons," she explains unapologetically.

Bella nods understandingly. "I go to underground fight nights. My demon revels in it."

"Anyway, so long story short, we crashed this wedding, but within minutes, we saw the women who made her day miserable yesterday, and then the man who made mine memorable." She laughs when Carter fidgets uncomfortably. "Glory wanted to bail, but I wouldn't let her. In the process of trying to avoid bitch face there" —she nods at Nicole— "she ended up mated to him." She points to Nolan. "But it looks like Nolan is already mated and, well, it was just too much. Hence the mental breakdown you witnessed." Serena waves down a passing waiter and grabs two glasses of fruity cocktails, handing one to me before she takes a sip. "And that is how we all came to be sitting here."

"Wait!" Louis exclaims. "Mated to Nolan?"

Nolan nods, still looking a bit shell-shocked.

"Congratulations, man." Louis and Carter both shake Nolan's hand, but their reactions seem a little off.

"Of course," I scoff. "He's the man, a second mate. Woo-hoo." I toss back my cocktail. This is not the time for dainty drinking. In fact… I signal to one of the waiters. "Tequila! Bring the bottle, lemons, and salt." He scurries away.

The guys all eye me warily, but Bella sighs deeply.

"Glory, Nolan isn't already mated. He was trapped in a relationship with the girls' human mother. She's gone now."

I look at him. "Trapped? Okay, I'd accept that the first time. What happened the second time? He tripped and fell into her vagina?"

He shakes his head, wearing a look of utter sadness on his face, then he takes a deep breath. "I tried to make the best of a bad situation. I wanted to make things work, and they didn't. When I tried to leave, she threatened to take Aria and not let me see her. I gave in. We were basically living separate lives in the same house. She was neglectful, and she had a vicious drug and alcohol problem, and after a while, I finally had enough proof that she was an unfit mother. I told her I was leaving and taking Aria with me when she drugged me. One night, I had a few too many drinks after work, and she slipped a cocktail of drugs into my meal and basically raped me. I wasn't in my right mind to consent, that's for sure."

He shudders, and Bella grabs his hand, giving it a squeeze as he continues. "Zoe was the result of that. I went to the police, but it was hard to prove, and the case was dropped. I'm not proud of what I did, but in the end, I paid her to go away. It's the only reason she was with me in the first place. I never planned to marry her or have children. I knew I had a mate out there, but I'm a wealthy man, and she manipulated the situation to her advantage. I made sure she couldn't touch them again. I love my girls, and I don't regret them one bit." He ends the story defensively.

"Are you saying there is no other woman in this relationship?" I ask, gesturing between us. He shakes his head. "I get to have you all to myself?"

This time he nods, laughing. "Well, you have to share me with my girls. That's nonnegotiable."

I launch myself out of my chair and into his lap, plastering little kisses all over his face before licking from the bottom of his cheek to his temple. His facial hair is rough against my tongue as I drag it across his face.

Nolan screws up his nose. "What was that for?" he asks, wiping at where I licked him.

Serena is just about falling off her chair with laughter. "She licked it. It belongs to her now."

Everyone else at the table dissolves into laughter, except B1 and B2, who turn up their noses and huff.

Chapter Six

Sometime later, Bella and Felix return to their guests, and Serena disappears to find a willing sexual partner. Out of the corner of my eye, I see Bella introducing her to someone, so I think she's going to be okay. The rest have given us a little bit of privacy, with Carter and Louis physically manhandling Nicole and Jenny when they wouldn't leave.

Nolan and I have been getting to know each other. He's a wrath demon who is independently wealthy, but he invests in promising startup companies like Tasty Treats, though that one was a bonus because it was with his best friends.

His little girls keep returning to the table from where they have been playing. They obviously don't like to let their daddy out of their sight for too long. It's adorable how close the three of them are. Hopefully, having me around won't mess with that dynamic too much. I can't wait to do stuff with them.

"Glory, are you going to live with us now? Are you going to be my mommy?" the little one, Zoe, asks.

I look at Nolan for guidance, but he just shrugs.

"They know about demons. We've never hidden anything. They also knew that one day, Daddy would find his soulmate and fall instantly in love." My heart skips a beat, and my eyes mist over slightly. "Aria understands more than Zoe, but Zoe has always asked when her mommy was going to be coming."

Turning to the sweet girl standing in front of me, I cautiously answer, "Is that okay with you?"

A huge grin spreads across her face, and she jumps up and down on the spot before climbing up onto my lap and wrapping her small arms around me. "Yes, yes, a gazillion times, yes!"

My arms come up automatically, and I hug her back. I inhale her little kid scent. Her hair smells like apples, and her cheek is sticky where it presses against mine. An instant feeling of love for this little cherub who's never known a mother's love flows through me. I will have to be very careful how I tread with these two and make sure they know I will love them as much as I love their father.

Aria tugs on her dad's hand. "Come dance with me, please."

At her plea, he looks at me.

I smile. "Nolan, you never have to ask my permission to spend time with your daughters."

He winks at me and stands up. "Let's go then, chipmunk." They head to the dance floor together.

When she climbs onto his shoes, and they slow dance together, I lose my heart a little bit more.

Zoe has made herself comfortable on my lap, and now she turns to me, placing her hand on my cheek. "You'll like living with us, Glory. We have a big house with a heated pool and a slide. We have lots of rooms. Aria and I each have a bedroom. Carter has a bedroom, Louis has a bedroom, and Daddy has a bedroom, and he has a humongous bed! He and Carter and Louis can all fit in it together!" She waves her arms around enthusiastically.

Wow. I'm speechless. There are so many things I have questions about, but I'm not going to pump a three-year-old for more information. Well, not much anyway.

Before I can ask any questions, though, the two men I'm curious about return to the table.

"Wow, Nolan left you all alone already?" Carter asks me. "I thought he would have been all over you. He's always talking about what his mate would be like. I guess you don't live up to the dream."

Carter's hostile words surprise me, and I'm not sure what the fuck I did to cause him to be so aggressive. Louis gives him a look that clearly says *shut up*, but Carter doesn't take the hint. He starts to spew what I'm sure is more nastiness, but Zoe distracts him by jumping down off my lap and grabbing his hand.

"Uncle Carter, come and dance with me, please? Like Aria and Daddy."

The scowl on his face melts off, and he dissolves into a puddle of mush. "Of course I will, my little cupcake," he says, picking her up and swinging her around. When they get to the dance floor, he keeps her in his arms and sways back and forth. She nestles her head into his shoulder and sticks her thumb in her mouth. This brings a smile to my face, but I turn so he can't see it.

Louis is looking at me with a small smile of his own. "He's right, you know. Nolan has looked forward to finding his mate for so long. He always wanted a huge family. It was the only reason he didn't tell his ex to take a hike. She knew pregnancy was the only thing that would trap him." He takes a seat in the vacant chair next to me. His cologne, something spicy and exotic, drifts past my nose, messing with my mind. I shake my head to clear it. "And don't mind Carter. He's jealous, but he'll come around."

I watch the four of them on the dance floor, the two men protective of the little girls they dance with.

"Zoe said some interesting things to me," I say to Louis.

He crosses one leg over the other and raises an eyebrow. "Did she now? *Mon petit* is subject to frequent exaggeration, but tell me, and I will tell you whether her tale is tall or not." His accent thickens on the French words.

"She said you guys have bedrooms at her house. Do you all live together?"

"Yes, we do. I guess Carter and I should look at getting our own place now if you are moving in."

I look at him shrewdly. "She also said that her daddy's bed was so big, 'Daddy and Louis and Carter all fit in it together.' How would she know that?"

He looks me in the eye, his irises flaring with the orange of a fellow gluttony demon. "Unfortunately, Zoe is not only an exaggerator, but she is also a sleep-walker. The sneaky girl woke one night and entered her father's bedroom. Luckily, she was asleep and didn't see anything too bad, but she does remember all three of us in bed. She thinks that we were having a slumber party." He gives me a slight frown. "Does it matter to you that your mate is bisexual? Well, I guess now that you are together, he will leave us behind, so you don't have to worry about us," he says sadly.

I think about what he just told me. Holy hotcakes, that visual just lit my undies on fire. I feel a little guilty thinking about men other than my mate, but whoa. I fan my face with a napkin from the table. As the evening settled in, the weather cooled off, but I can feel my face flaming, and I wiggle in my seat.

"He's a very lucky man." He lifts his hand to

push back a tendril of hair from my face. As he does, his palm brushes across my cheek, and a sharp, stabbing pain flares in my hand.

I gasp and look down for an injury. My demon symbol, which was orange with a red ring after I mated with Nolan, has changed again. There is now an orange ring around the red one. I look up in shock. Louis is also stunned, and he's holding his hand out. His demon mark has turned from black to orange.

"Mate?" he questions.

I shrug and nod, my mouth hanging open in surprise. He grabs me and hauls me to him, slamming his lips onto mine as he kisses me like a man starved for air.

My heart races and my core quivers with desire. He tastes like sunshine and rainbows, sweet and surprising, as his tongue licks mine, sampling and savoring. I return the kiss with as much fervor. Immediately, a ton of guilt slams into me, and I pull away, spinning to look at Nolan on the dance floor. He has left Aria with Carter and is approaching with a face like a thundercloud, his fists clenched.

"My own fucking best friend! What the hell?" he spits out, the fury evident in his tone.

Louis holds up his hand, showing his demon mark. "Nolan, wait, she is mine too, *oui*."

Nolan skids to a stop, his expression shifting from anger to surprise to absolute delight. He pulls Louis into his arms and hugs him. If I didn't already know of their relationship, the intimacy of this hug would have told me everything I needed. You would think jealousy would roll through me at the thought, but the images it creates just causes my panties to flood with excitement.

I sit back down, unstable on my feet as they both turn to me. Two mates, wow! Twice as much fun. I didn't think I would end up with two!

Smiling, I watch as they examine each other's demon marks. Both have my ring around their own color, but they also now have each other's too. So many questions flood my mind. Are we all mates? Not just me and them, but them with each other too? And if so, then why didn't the marks change color before now?

I look beyond the two men and see Carter with the girls, still on the dance floor. He is doing an excellent job of keeping them distracted, but I can tell by the look of devastation on his face that he knows what happened.

The song ends, and the girls run back toward us. Carter turns and walks in the opposite direction. Nolan and Louis are looking between us, and the indecision on their faces is heartbreaking.

"Go," I tell them. "He needs you. I can't be selfish. He will end up resenting us all."

They turn and hurry after him. The girls watch them go, so I stand up and grab their hands. "Let's check out the dessert table. Dessert is my favorite thing." The girls giggle, and we weave our way toward the buffet.

"Dessert is Louis's favorite too. He makes yummy things," Aria tells me.

I stop suddenly as I realize I am mated to the man who made all those yummy treats.

I throw my hand in the air, fist-pump style, and then start doing a little happy dance, twerking on the spot. The girls watch with delight, and Zoe joins in, her little body trying to twerk but looking more like she's having an epileptic fit. I am so happy right now. I wave at Aria, and she joins in too. All three of us are twerking like sorority girls at a frat party. Serena comes over and joins us. Before we know it, we are surrounded by twerking, drunk, giggling women. The DJ has changed the music, and it's turning into a dance party.

Sometime later, I'm hot and my body is starting to ache. I realize I need to eat again, so I drag Zoe and Aria out from the crowd, and we continue to the buffet, Serena following behind us.

"What was that all about?" she asks. She has a glow on her face that isn't from that little bit of dancing. I must get the deets later.

The girls grab a plate and start to pile on desserts. Typical little demons. Hungry all the time. Even though their traits won't kick in until puberty, the hunger is already there. Who am I to say anything?

"Oh, I just realized that I'm mated to the man

who made all the desserts I ate yesterday," I tell Serena. "So I was celebrating."

"What, Nolan made them? I thought it was Louis." She scratches her head in confusion.

Putting down my plate, I spin, grab her hands, and jump up and down in excitement. "I have two mates. Nolan and Louis."

Her eyes widen in surprise, then narrow in suspicion. "Well, where are they then?"

"I have so much to tell you. Let's get these and go find a table, then I'll fill you in."

After loading up on desserts and coffee, we find a table and indulge in the decadence. While we do, I quietly tell Serena what happened—not that I need to worry about the girls, since they are engrossed in the sugary goodness in front of them.

At the end of the story, she flops back against her chair. "You lucky bitch. That sounds hot." I see her look to the sky and mumble a few words under her breath.

"What was that?" I ask.

"That was a prayer to the big man above to bless me like he has you." She wraps her arms around me and gives me a huge hug. "I am so happy for you, Glory."

I hug her in return. I'm so happy too. I just hope the guys can sort everything out with Carter.

Chapter Seven

After finishing our delicious desserts, the girls drag Serena back to the dance floor. Watching her teach Zoe and Aria how to dance to "Macarena" is adorable. Aria has it, but Zoe is struggling. Serena is patient, however, and eventually, the girls get the hang of it.

I scan the crowd, noticing it has slowly started to thin out. The older guests have left, and only the young ones continue to party into the night. Toward the back, I catch sight of Nolan, Louis, and Carter on the other side of the garden. The threesome appears to be involved in an intense conversation.

This isn't what I thought would happen when I first met my mate. I thought we wouldn't be able to keep our hands off each other. It never occurred to me that they would already be involved with someone.

Sighing, I turn back toward the dance floor. The DJ is playing "Macarena" one more time, and the girls are having a blast. A shadow appears out of the corner of my eye, and Bella collapses into the chair next to me, her dress rustling in complaint.

"God, I've had enough! Can I leave yet?" She nudges a shoe off and lifts her foot to rub the arch, groaning in relief.

I smile at her and nod. "You're the bride! That makes you the boss, doesn't it? You don't need to be here for people to have fun. The manor will kick them out when their time is up."

She sits up straighter, a look of relief crossing her face. "Yeah, you're right. I want to go home and bang my husband's brains out." She looks around. "Where's Nolan? I need to say goodbye. Everyone else can suck it."

I swivel in my seat to where I know the guys are. The conversation looks like it has escalated, with angry faces and furious gestures.

Bella follows my gaze and nods in that direction. "What is that about?"

Oh God. She's a wrath demon! Do I really want to tell her that I'm mated to more than her brother?

"Ah, it turns out Louis is my mate too." I wince, expecting the worst.

Instead, her face lights up, and she grabs my hand in excitement. "Oh, that's amazing! I was worried about how they were going to cope."

"You know about them?" I ask in surprise.

"Yes, they've been together on and off for a long time. When Nolan was trapped by his ex, he let them go because he was trying to do the right thing, but they picked up again when she was out of the picture. They have all had other partners and regularly date others, like those bitches. Carter especially needed more since he's a lust demon, but they all gravitate back to each other." Her expression falls at the mention of Carter, and her head swivels around to watch them. "Oh no, poor Carter."

My heart drops. This is not good. I feel like I'm a home-wrecker breaking up a happy, healthy relationship.

She turns back, pasting a smile on her face, but when she goes to say something, I hold my hand up, stopping her.

"No, Bella. It's a clusterfuck. It seems like the theme of the day." I pull my card out of my clutch and hand it to her. "Can you watch the girls while Nolan is busy? I'm going to grab Serena and make our way home." I kiss her cheek. "I'd apologize for crashing your wedding, but I'm really not sorry. Tell Nolan and Louis to give me a call when they sort their shit out."

She nods then grabs my clutch and pulls out my phone. After putting in her number, she sends a text to herself, then returns it to the purse. "We now have each other's number." Smiling, she puts her hand over mine. "Call me if you need to. Anytime. We aren't having a honeymoon right away. Felix organized a big exhibit that's currently showing and, well, he's too much of a pride demon to give that up. Oh, I'm so happy Nolan found you. You are going to be so good for that family."

Picking up my clutch and waving goodbye, I head to the dance floor to grab Serena. She and the girls moved on from "Macarena" and are now doing some kind of line dance thing.

I pull the girls to the side. "I'm going home now. Aunty Bella is over there waiting for you," I tell them, pointing her out.

Zoe's bottom lip wobbles, and tears build in her eyes. "I thought you were coming home with us. You said you would be my mommy."

My heart plummets into my stomach. Crouching down, I pull her in for a hug. "Oh, honey. I'm sure at one stage I will, but I live with Serena right now. All my things are at our place. It takes some time for us to be able to move. I need to speak to your daddy, and he's a little busy at the moment." I pull back and look at her. "I will see you soon, okay? Aunty Bella has my number, and you can call me whenever you want."

She nods, and Aria grabs her hand, pulling her away. Tears build in my eyes, but I don't want to make any promises I can't keep. After giving them both kisses, I walk away, letting tears flow down my cheeks once I know they can't see them.

So much has happened in such a short period of time. I have two mates and two beautiful little girls who already have my heart. I also gained a possible new friend in the form of Bella. I made two definite enemies in the form of Nicole and Jenny and, very possibly, Carter, I realize. My heart is heavy for him, but for me too. I know it's selfish, but I really don't think I can share them with him. The possessiveness has kicked in, even though the bond hasn't been sealed.

"Don't be sad, Glowworm." Serena hip-bumps me. "Everything will work itself out."

I shake my head at her as we wander off in search of a taxi. "I really don't want to talk about or think about it. Distract me," I demand. "Tell me about your booty call. You were gone for a while."

She looks at me with a wicked grin on her face. "Bella's bridesmaid Lizzie and her husband are both lust demons. It's just the pair of them in their mating, so they agreed to add others to their sex life to feed. It's strange how that worked out and very unusual," she muses.

I nudge her to get her attention, and she shakes her head and continues.

"Anyway, the rules are that they must agree on who, and it has to be together. No going off on their own. Let's just say the three of us fed very well this evening." She gets a dreamy look in her eyes. "They both have some mad sex skills. The things Lizzie could do with her tongue made my toes curl, and her hubby's cock… If I was dancing funny, he was the reason why." She bursts out into peals of laughter, and I join in.

This is just the distraction I need.

"Seriously, though, I wouldn't mind if they asked me to join them again. I fed better than I did yesterday with Mr. Big... uh, I mean Carter," she finishes awkwardly, looking at me and mouthing, "Sorry."

I roll my eyes. "Don't! I just can't." Walking quickly ahead, I flag down a taxi that just pulled up in front of the manor before anyone else can. I climb in and give the driver our address, waiting for Serena to jump in too.

Pulling the door shut, she turns to me and pats my leg. "Things will seem better in the morning."

We sit silently for the entire trip home, both of us lost in our own thoughts, although I'm sure hers are a lot more exciting than mine.

As soon as we arrive home, Serena takes off to her bedroom to change, but I can't find the energy to do the same. Instead, I throw myself on the couch and turn the TV to some random program for background noise. My mind is tumultuous with so many scenarios running around in it.

What if they decide they don't want to be with me? What if they want to continue having a relationship with Carter as well as me? My anger rises at the thought.

What if they want me to have a relationship with Carter as well?

The rising anger rapidly turns to lust, and I roll my eyes at my slutty inner demon. The idea of having one more man added to the mix drives the gluttonous bitch wild. Apparently we can't be happy with two when we could have three.

Rolling onto my stomach, I bury my face into the cushion and scream in frustration.

"You know, there are easier ways to do yourself in," Serena says.

I flip her off and stay where I am, happy to pretend I'm in a safe cocoon where nothing can go wrong.

"Grow up, Glory, you have to face this," she scolds, reaching down and unlacing the ribbons on my shoes and removing them from my feet. She then smacks my legs, wanting me to give her room, and shoves her body into the space.

"Not tonight, I don't," I mumble around the cushion.

"Come on. I got you something to eat."

"What?" Curiosity gets the better of me.

"You're going to have to sit up to find out."

Damn it! The sneaky bitch knows I won't turn down food.

I sit up, and to my delight, there is a loaded pizza on the table. Surprised, I ask her, "Where did that come from?"

She smiles affectionately at me. "Honey, I know what you're like. I ordered it in the taxi on the way home from my phone. The driver just delivered it."

Looking in the direction of the door, I realize I was so lost in my own little world, I didn't even hear the doorbell ring. I reach for a piece and shovel it into my mouth. The cheesy, meaty goodness explodes on my tongue, and I practically purr with delight.

This is getting ridiculous. I need to get the feeding issue sorted, pronto.

I put the slice down. "Serena, although I appreciate the pizza, food isn't going to fix this clusterfuck of a situation. I don't understand. I thought the mating thing was a done deal and that they wouldn't feel the need for anyone else, but that clearly isn't right. I could tell Louis and Nolan both feel something for each other and Carter."

She frowns at me. "I thought the same thing, but Lizzie and Jake were like that this evening too. They said they regularly have to have others in their bed. It's like something or someone is missing. Both commented afterward that it was the fullest they'd felt in a long time. They have been together six years, and they have sex with other people almost every day. I gave them my card. I told them to come in, and we could set up an account. It must be exhausting having to pick up singles and strangers all the time." She picks up her phone and taps a couple of things, then lays it on the table. "Let's ask Mom."

The phone rings a few times, then my mom's husky voice comes out of the speaker. "Reni, I was just talking to your fathers about you girls."

"Hi, Mom. Glory's here too."

Grunting, I continue to shovel pizza into my mouth.

"Goodness, I can hear her eating over the phone. What has she been doing to cause such a feeding frenzy?"

"Oh, Mom," Serena says, "I have so much to tell you." While I continue stuffing my face, Serena tells her all about our last two days. She shares a few too many details of her encounter with Lizzie and Jake, if you ask me, but lust demons are a different kind of breed, so I just ignore it and polish off a few more slices of pizza.

"We were just wondering if you know what's going on, Mom."

Mom sighs loudly. "Girls, I knew you weren't listening to half of what I told you. Yes, the mating bond should override any other attraction, but only once it has been sealed by all parties involved in the mating. Sometimes it fails to show unless all people in the mating are in contact. Now that they've found Glory, the mate marks are free to form."

She takes a deep breath. "Glory, honey, you're going to have to suck it up and talk it out with your fellows, especially with two little girls being involved." She squeals suddenly. "Grandchildren! We have grandbabies." She must have put the phone down, because all we can hear is her muffled shouting to the dads that they have grandbabies.

"You hang that thing up, and you do it now," I

hiss at Serena as I point at the phone. "I do not need to deal with all that tonight."

She does as I ask and hangs up the phone, leaning back in the chair and giving me a look.

Again, I shake my head. "Just give me tonight, please!"

She smiles sadly and watches as I pick up my shoes and wander off to my room.

Washing the makeup from my face, I tie my hair into a bun, pull off my dress, and then crawl into my cold, empty bed. I wrap my arms around my body and pray for a dreamless sleep. It comes, but not before I spend hours tossing and turning.

Once the light starts to peek over the horizon, I finally fall into a restless sleep.

Chapter Eight

My phone obnoxiously blares out Taylors Swift's "Shake It Off," abruptly waking me the next morning. I hit decline. Five seconds later, it rings again, and I decline it as well. When it rings a third time, I pick it up, get out of bed, and toss it down the hall. A crash and a screech from Serena reaches my ears, but I have no fucks left to give as I shut the door. Going back to bed, I climb in and pull up the quilt, shoving my head under the pillow. Taylor can kiss my ass this morning, and so can whoever the hell it is who's trying to call me.

Sometime later, I'm floating in that space between consciousness and sleep, drifting happily. It's not until my bedroom door opens, bouncing off the bedroom wall, that I realize the voice isn't that bitch Taylor telling me to shake it off again. After hearing a grunt followed by a "Fuck" in a voice much deeper than my sister's, I roll over to see who it is.

Nolan stands there, his expression thunderous, and he's on fire. Orange and blue flames lick up and down his body.

I rub my eyes, wondering if I am still dreaming, and give myself a pinch. Nope, definitely awake. I stare at him in surprise. "How did you find me? What are you doing here?" My tired brain is having trouble understanding what's happening.

"You left!" he growls. "I have been on fire since I realized you left without me. Without talking to us. You just left."

Anger rises inside my chest. "Fuck you, Nolan. You and Louis were too busy trying to talk Carter down to give a fuck about me, so I left. I don't answer to you or him or anyone."

"You told us to go."

I throw my hands up in frustration. "I didn't expect you to stay gone!"

His eyes widen through the flames, and they start to glow red. I follow his gaze and realize that when I threw my hands up, I also lost my blanket, and my girls are saying good morning to Nolan. Apparently, his morning is starting to look up. Huffing, I get up and grab a robe from the back of my bathroom door.

"I thought you would talk him down and return to me. I waited for two hours. Excuse me for being petty, but I thought becoming mated would go way differently than it actually did. I thought Bella wasn't the only one who was going to get her brains banged out last night. My mom always made being mated seem so magical, but you know what? She lied. Big fat lie."

Tying the robe closed, I slide past Nolan and walk to the kitchen. For some reason, he doesn't seem to be setting the floor on fire, but it seems like a smart idea to stand on a tiled floor just in case.

I grab a cup and stick it under the coffee machine, then hit the start button. The machine's loud grinding drowns out any possible chance to talk. Pity I can't just keep pressing the button all day. Once it's finished its cycle, I add a teaspoon of sugar, and then take it to the fridge for milk. All the while, Nolan stands there, flickering with flames. I am rolling in laughter on the inside. Let the bastard suffer. I splash a bit of milk in and take a long, needed gulp. A low growl sounds out.

"Glory, please," he pleads, "I haven't slept. I'm exhausted. The girls need me."

Whoa, that's a low blow, using the girls.

"Oh, boo-hoo, you big baby," Serena says, entering the kitchen.

Rolling my eyes, I put my cup down on the bench then hold my hands out to him, gesturing for him to hold them. He grabs on like they are a life preserver, and he's a drowning sailor. After we take a few deep breaths as one, the flames slowly flicker before disappearing altogether. He sinks down onto another stool.

"Thank you." He sounds grateful, but I couldn't give a shit. I pick my coffee up and head back to my room.

"You can leave now," I hear Serena tell him

before I close my bedroom door and lock it behind me.

Running the shower at Satan's big toe temperatures, I wait for steam to fill the room before climbing in. Wrapped in a cloudy, foggy shroud, I pretend the world doesn't exist—or I try to, but some fucker is banging on my door again. Arggghhh!

I slam the shower open and reach for a towel before wrapping it around my body and wrenching the bathroom door open. "What do you want, Nolan? I think we've established that I'm pissed at you."

Growling, he pulls me, wet and dripping, toward his hard body. "You are mine!" His eyes are glowing red, indicating his wrath demon is in full control. "Pack up your shit. You're coming home with me. Now."

Whoa! Wrathful Nolan is fucking hot. I feel a flood of desire in my lower regions, but I'm not sure how I feel about this. On one hand, I want to throw myself at his feet and tell him to take me any way he wants. On the other hand, I was really hurt by what happened last night.

His eyes shift back to their normal green color, and he takes a deep breath. "Please, Glory. We have a lot to talk about, and the girls would love to see you again. Zoe cried herself to sleep last night, and Aria wouldn't speak to us at all."

The desire evaporates, and my anger explodes.

"Don't you try to use emotional blackmail against me," I grind out as I poke him in the chest. "That was all your fault, douchebag. I was fully prepared to go home with you last night, so that's all on you, buddy."

Slamming the door in his face, I finish my shower before drying myself off. I dress in some yoga pants and a hoodie I had in the bathroom. There's no underwear, unfortunately, but I don't really care at this stage. When I return to my bedroom, I lose my shit. Nolan is standing by the bed with my suitcase open on top, and my room looks like a tornado has been through it. There is stuff littered from one end of the room to the other.

"What in Satan's underpants are you doing?" I ask him.

He ignores me and keeps throwing things in the suitcase.

"No, seriously, what are you doing?" I demand with my hands on my hips.

Again, he ignores me, zips the suitcase shut, and disappears out the door with it. Speechless, I walk out to the kitchen.

Serena's sitting there drinking a cup of coffee, her laptop open. She looks up. "What's up with that?" She nods toward the front door where Nolan just went, taking my suitcase with him.

"No fucking idea. I haven't eaten, and he interrupted my sleep, coffee, and shower. At the moment, he is lucky I don't own a gun." I open the fridge to see what we have for breakfast, and a screech escapes my mouth as my feet leave the ground. I'm being carried through the door like a football, folded in half like a fucking pretzel. Profanities fly from my mouth in fury as I struggle in vain.

"I told you. You are mine, and I'm not leaving without what's mine," he growls at me as he shoves me in his car. Serena laughs from the front door, so I flip her off.

"Fuck you, bitch!" I continue trying to escape, but Nolan engages the child lock so I can't get the door open.

Serena doubles over laughing and waves back. "You might want to feed her, Nolan. Otherwise, she'll continue to be a rabid dog!"

"I know where you fucking live!" I shout as he drives off.

I sit sullenly with my arms crossed, ignoring him. I'm like a toddler who hasn't gotten their way. He doesn't seem to mind though. Nolan turns on the radio and starts to sing along.

I'm silently plotting his murder and where I'm going to hide his body when he starts talking.

"We didn't mean to hurt you, Glory. Once we realized you left, we recognized how our actions could have been interpreted. Bella reamed us both out. Her wrath demon was in its element, feeding deeply. I bet Felix got a workout last night." He screws his face up. "Gross! I can't believe I said that."

This elicits a smile from me, but I quickly wipe it off as he continues.

"Anyway, we're sorry. Louis has been cooking for you all morning. He thought some good food would go a long way toward making things up to you, especially since you're struggling with your energy."

My curiosity is piqued. I turn to look at his handsome profile, and I can just make out an upturned lip on one side of his mouth. "Back the truck up, buddy," I tell him. "Don't get ahead of yourself. You're not out of the doghouse yet."

A smile crosses his whole face, and he turns and winks at me. "I'm pretty sure I know a way I can make it up to you fully." He starts to whistle as we continue to drive.

Sometime later, we pull into a neighborhood with huge houses. The yards are pristine, with golf green worthy lawns, trimmed hedges, and immaculate garden beds. Many are surrounded by large, wrought iron fences with elaborate gated entries. We get to the end of a dead-end street with another gated entrance. This gate is wide open, and Nolan drives through. My mouth drops open in surprise as we drive down the leafy, tree-lined driveway. There are cute, little old-fashioned streetlamps scattered between the trees that must light up the driveway at night. As we approach the house, my mouth snaps closed. The house is enormous, with lots of large glass windows that must let in a considerable amount of natural light.

I shake my head. "I hope you know I don't do windows."

He just smiles as he brings the car to a stop. "I have someone come and do the windows," he assures me before jumping out and coming around to my side to open the door for me.

Hopping out, I stare wide-eyed at the house before me. It's like someone took my Pinterest page and made it real. I walk to the balustrade of the stone steps and run my hand over the smooth wood. There isn't a catch or splinter in sight, even though the wood is exposed to the elements.

Nolan walks past with my suitcase and pushes open the front door, shouting, "We're home!"

I follow him up and into the house. Noise erupts as two little girls come running down a circular staircase to the right side of the entrance. Zoe jumps from the last step and throws her arms around me. Grunting, I catch her little body, and the smell of apples surrounds me. Aria is not quite as enthusiastic, but she does give me a shy smile and grabs one of my hands.

"I missed you so very much, Glory," Zoe whispers in my ear. "Daddy has been a real poofberry since last night."

Aria nods, and I smother a smile at the description.

"He kept burning things," Aria tells me. "He had to stay outside once we got home because Uncle Louis didn't want him to burn the house down, but he did burn down four pool lounges, and the backyard smells like burning plastic." She wrinkles her nose in disgust.

"Yeah," Zoe chimes in. "Uncle Carter says we're getting wooden chairs next time because they won't stink if they burn up."

I look awkwardly at Nolan at the mention of Carter.

He gestures for us to follow him. "Come on, let's go see what Uncle Louis is doing in the kitchen."

Zoe whoops and jumps down from my arms, disappearing in the same direction as Nolan.

Aria keeps hold of my hand and tugs me forward. "I'll show you where the kitchen is."

I must look like a tourist, my mouth gaping open as I take in the house. Aria lets me look my fill but gets impatient, dragging me toward another doorway. Walking into the kitchen, I see a sight that fills my heart with love and joy and makes all my dreams come true.

ria leaves me and moves away. The kitchen is a chef's delight, but the island is what draws my attention. It's covered in macarons from one end to the other. The shiny, colorful little pieces of joy look like sparkly precious jewels in a pirate's treasure. My heart sings, my stomach rumbles, and my head puts on the brakes, skidding my emotions to a halt. Looking up, I see Nolan and Louis staring at me with hopeful expressions.

I put my hands on my hips and adopt a mien of disdain. "Damn you and your macarons of mass seduction. It's a shame that I cannot be bought." When I see their faces drop, I let them off the hook slightly. "But it's a start."

Their expressions lift again as I walk over and sit down at the island with the girls. I look over the array, tapping my finger on my chin. I just don't know where to start.

Zoe tugs on my hoodie. "Look at these, Glory. I picked these. They are unicorn macarons," she says excitedly.

"Wow, Zoe, they look awesome! I can't wait to try one." I smile at her joy.

Aria tugs on my hand and gestures to a pale green one, filled with what looks like chocolate. "These are my favorite, Glory, mint chocolate chip, and those are Dad's, and those are Uncle Carter's." She points out a yellow macaron and a dark pink one that has chocolate filling. "They are lemon curd and raspberry chocolate."

My stomach rumbles again. So many delicious flavors! I can't wait to get started. I look up at Louis. "And which is your favorite?"

A small smile crosses his lips. He walks closer to me and leans over, his chest brushing against my shoulder. A tingle runs through me that isn't related to hunger.

Louis pulls over a plate of pale cream-colored macarons. "These. They are vanilla bean and caramelized white chocolate with chili buttercream. They may look innocent, but on the inside, they pack a punch," he whispers in my ear.

I wiggle on my seat. Damn it. I regret not putting underwear on now.

He straightens back up. "But you can't eat the macarons yet," he tells me as he walks over to the oven.

My stomach roars its disappointment, and everyone looks at me in shock.

"I'm ravenous!" I tell them, shrugging sheepishly.

The girls dissolve into giggles, and Nolan chuckles, while Louis grabs an oven mitt and pulls a plate out of the oven.

"Breakfast first," he says, depositing it in front of me with a flourish.

My heart melts a little further. In front of me is a plate that would make a weight watcher have a heart attack. Eggs Benedict, with smoked ham and crusty bread, sits next to sautéed mushrooms, grilled tomatoes, and hash browns. He sets another plate in front of me piled high with fluffy pancakes with banana slices and syrup on top. The last dish is a breakfast burrito. While Louis handled the food, Nolan made me a cup of coffee.

"Go on, Glory, eat!" Zoe shouts, so I do.

The girls keep me entertained the whole time with stories about their school friends, what sports they play, what their favorite food is, and their favorite TV program. My taste buds are exploding. Louis truly is a master chef. I stop eating and shoot a little prayer up, then turn and shoot one down. I'm not sure who is responsible, but I wouldn't want to thank the wrong deity.

Louis and Nolan have disappeared, and it's like the girls were asked to distract me, because they chatter nonstop. I finally finish my feast and decide to grab another cup of coffee. Walking over to the coffee machine, I stick my cup under and press a button then wait while the coffee is made.

I turn around, and I'm tackled by a huge, hairy

monster. It takes me to the ground, snarling at me with its enormous teeth as it pins me with its furry body. My life flashes before my eyes.

I struggle to get it off me, but it's almost as big as I am. "Help! Help! It's going to eat me!" I cry feebly, spitting fur out of my mouth.

The girls laugh as they grab hold of the monster by a collar, trying to pull it off.

Collar?

Looking again, I see two odd eyes staring at me, one blue and one brown. Then, before I can do anything else, it licks me from one side of my cheek to the other. Its huge tongue is covered in slobber, and its warm breath takes away my own with its smell.

"He licked you, so does that mean he owns you?" a deep, husky voice asks from somewhere behind the monster.

Giggling, the girls manage to pull the monster off me and make him sit. Struggling back to my feet, I see what I now know is a big dog. It's a fluffy, wolf-colored creature. A husky maybe? It's pretty big, so perhaps it's an Alaskan malamute. Standing behind him, wearing nothing but jogging shorts and shoes, is Carter.

"Girls, your dad is looking for you. Your friend is here to take you to the park for a couple of hours."

The girls let go of the monster/wolf/dog that

wanders over to a dog bowl and takes vast gulps of water. They wave goodbye, telling me they'll be back later, and disappear out the door. I wave goodbye but keep an eye on the monster/wolf/dog. He flops down on the floor, closing his eyes and panting softly.

Is this real, or is it trying to lull me into a false sense of security?

Tiptoeing just in case, I grab my cup of coffee from the machine and put it on the counter. I turn to get milk and just about smack into Carter, who has moved closer. I look up at him. He's so much taller than me. My eyes drift to his broad shoulders and bulging biceps. His pecs are well-defined and lead down to washboard abs that I would have once loved to have run my tongue over. He has a small trail of hair from his belly button down into his shorts, but apart from that, his chest is hairless. His running shorts don't leave much to the imagination, and my eyes quickly skim by out of respect for my mates.

"Are you finished eye-fucking me, or are two mates not enough for you?"

My gaze shoots back to his face in shock, and so does my hand as it cracks across his cheek with a force that leaves a red mark on both him and my hand.

"Fuck you!" I shout at him. "Can't you just be happy for them, you jealous prick?" As I shake out my hand, I realize that he's staring at me in shock, and then I recognize that the pain in my hand is not from slapping him, but from another colored ring forming around my demon mark.

"No! Oh, no." I gape at him.

He is looking down at his hand. His demon mark is now dark blue, and so is the ring around mine. Our eyes meet. Where his eyes were icy and cruel seconds earlier, they are now burning with heat and fire.

"Well, fuck me," I mutter quietly.

"Oh, baby, when I'm done with you, you won't be able to walk straight for a week."

"Hold your horses and calm the farm, Romeo." I hold up my hand. "Do you really think that after that little performance, I'm going to drop my panties for you?"

He runs his hand through his hair, a sheepish look crossing his face. "Can you forgive a jealous fool? Please?"

Of course I can, but I'm going to make him sweat. I pretend to think about it, and a worried look creases his features. After counting to one hundred and watching a range of emotions cross his face, I can't leave him hanging.

"Okay, but you need to cut that shit out now. With four of us in this relationship, we're going to solve our issues by talking. Alright?"

He nods. I think he would have agreed to anything.

Before I can say anything else, he bends down and throws me over his shoulder. Shocked, I just hang there like a sack of sugar. He heads toward a staircase and makes his way up, not even puffing even though he's carrying my less than skinny body. I worry about him hurting himself, so I pound on his back.

"Put me down, I'm too heavy! You'll put your back out or have a hernia."

He just laughs and gives my ass a sharp slap, eliciting a string of profanities, to which he just laughs harder and gives it another slap, rubbing away the sting. Trapped and unable to move, I decide to just wait him out. I close my eyes, starting to feel nauseous from the movement after all that food. It wouldn't do for me to puke down my new mate's back, although it would be funny after all the grief he's given me. I contemplate opening my eyes, but we suddenly come to a stop.

He puts me down, and I find myself in an opulent bathroom. I see lots of gray and blue, but before I have a chance to look around, he's running the shower. It has a large rainfall showerhead in the ceiling and jets on the wall.

He strips down naked, his erect cock…

Oh my god!

Serena was not exaggerating. Before I can even blink, he has me out of my clothes—well, it's not like I was wearing much.

His eyes heat with desire and start to glow dark

blue. His lust demon has come out to play. "Want to get wet with me?"

"Too late," I say in my most seductive voice. "I already am."

Suddenly, our mouths are fused together in a violent explosion of passion. This man, who I have felt many different feelings for over the last twenty-four hours, is stoking a flame in my core like no other has before. Is this a mate thing? Maybe a lust demon thing? Would I have the same with Louis and Nolan as well? I've never felt like this before.

My body explodes into flames, and Carter quickly maneuvers us under the showerhead. The water instantly turns to steam when it hits my flaming body, fogging the shower walls. Not once have our mouths separated. Our tongues battle for dominance, but I feel like I'm losing the war. This man is a powerhouse of desire, and I just want to bathe in his prowess. Guilt starts to trickle in, so I pull my mouth back from his and push against his chest.

"I don't know about this. Maybe we should talk about it, or at least talk to Louis and Nolan," I tell him, gasping for air. His cock presses against my stomach, weakening my morals.

"I was a jealous idiot," he says, looking me in the eye. "I was scared of losing them, but also jealous that you were their mate. Forgive me?"

I nod, a bit breathless. "Good enough."

I slam my mouth onto a dusky brown, taut nipple, biting and sucking it before switching to the other side. Wrapping my hand around his thick rod of steel, I pump my fist up and down his length. He groans and drops his head to my shoulder as he thrusts his hips back and forth. My other hand fondles his sack, tugging and pulling on it, and dragging more sounds from him.

He shoves my hands away. "Enough," he growls, pushing me back against the tiles. He kneels, and with no warning, he sucks hard on my clit, thrusting two fingers in at the same time.

Holy shit. I say a little prayer to those deities again, thanking them for a man who doesn't mess around. His fingers are curled slightly and thrusting deep into my pussy while his tongue lashes my clit. My orgasm builds like a freight train that's out of control. I shudder with desire, and with one last hard suck, my body detonates.

"God fucking yes. Yes, yes, yes!"

He slows down to allow my body to adjust, but the orgasm just continues to flow, my body shaking and quivering with aftershocks as the flames die out. He places little kisses all the way up my body, paying particular attention to my nipples on the way past. I'm glad he did, because they were feeling a little left out. He gets to my mouth and gently kisses me.

"That's one," I tell him.

He pulls back and looks at me, confused.

"Well, Serena said you gave her four the other day," I explain. "Let's see how well you do today. You have a lot to make up for." I wink as I step out of the shower.

is mouth drops open in shock, and two loud shouts of laughter ring out. We spin around, finding Louis and Nolan standing in the bathroom doorway. I look between them and Carter, my heart pounding with anxiety.

"I can explain. He… and… we—" I stutter, but Nolan holds up his hand and points at his demon mark.

"We know. We felt it too." He steps closer and pulls me in for a kiss, then passes me to Louis, who also kisses me deeply. Breathless, I turn around to ask a question and find Nolan and a naked Carter wrapped around each other.

Oh my Satan's underpants. I feel a trickle down my leg, and it is not water from the shower.

"Last one naked and in bed is the caboose!" I smack Louis's ass and race toward the giant, double king-sized bed that's on a raised platform in the middle of the room. I scramble up the couple of steps leading to it, ignoring everything around me. There will be time for that after I get my mate sandwich.

I screech to a stop.

Hang on. There are four of us, so it can't be a sandwich. What's it called? Shaking my head, I throw myself on the bed. Who cares? I'll worry about it later.

Carter is right behind me. Of course, he's already naked. Both Louis and Nolan are stripping, and I ogle them without shame. Nolan is as well-built as Carter, but not quite as tall. Louis has more of a swimmer's body, lean with plenty of muscle definition. Looking at both their packages, I stand up on the bed and start twerking and dancing around. They stop what they are doing and look at me in surprise.

"What are you doing?" Louis asks, his accent thickening with his curiosity, his eyes heating with desire.

"I'm doing my happy dance. I totally get why the three of you always ended up together. Your cocks are amazing."

They look down, laugh, and keep struggling out of their clothes. Carter pulls me down on the bed. He snuggles into me, placing kisses on the crook of my neck and thrusting his cock against my hip. Our heads are down near the end of the bed, so I turn around and climb my way to the top, then slide my mouth down his cock, swallowing as much as I can. He grunts loudly, but I don't give him a chance to say anything as I present my pussy for him to feast on. He takes the hint, and this time he starts off slower, licking and sucking my folds before his tongue swirls and dips inside. It's so good that I struggle to pay attention to what I'm doing. I drag my mouth off his dick and run my tongue around the head like it's my favorite lollipop. He groans and thrusts up, never pausing in what he's doing.

Hmm, talented.

Just as I'm about to take him into my mouth again, I feel a smooth hand against my butt cheek.

"Open up, Carter, and get me wet for Glory," Nolan demands.

Stopping and turning, I watch as Carter pulls away from my pussy and opens his mouth wide, taking Nolan all the way down to the back of his throat. When Nolan pulls out, Carter runs his tongue around Nolan's head. I can see a line of saliva stretching from Nolan's cock to Carter's mouth.

Nolan leans down and kisses him. "Good boy. Scoot down a bit. I want her pussy."

Carter shifts slightly, and Nolan tilts my hips, giving me a small slap on the ass.

"Glory, be a good girl and suck Carter's dick," Nolan orders.

I turn back around, and just as I put my mouth over it, Nolan thrusts into my pussy. I gasp, and Carter shoves into my mouth, farther than I took him before. I'm unable to do anything but moan as they continue to thrust in and out, filling both my pussy and mouth. I feel my orgasm start to build, my body bucking as Carter's arms wrap around me to hold me still. Sweat beads across my skin, the small tingles evolving to a bright blaze of passion. I'm on the edge and just about to go over when I feel Louis reach between Carter and me. He caresses my breasts, and then pinches my nipples hard. Like a firework, my body detonates. I take my mouth off Carter and scream out in passion.

My pussy grips Nolan as he continues to thrust through my orgasm, once, twice, before he erupts with a shout of ecstasy. The pleasure starts to dissipate, but I feel a click as Nolan's mate bond snaps into place.

Nolan strokes his hands over my ass and thighs, whispering, "Such a good girl," and then he helps me roll off Carter.

"That's two," Carter tells me, sitting up.

I shake my head and wave him off. "Ah… no, buddy, that was all Nolan. You're still at one."

A look of determination settles on his face. "Challenge accepted." His cock is still rock hard and weeping from the end, his length glistening from my mouth. He plumps some pillows at the head of the bed and then reclines back. Nolan lies down next to him, fisting his cock in his hand as he lazily strokes it up and down.

Oh my god.

"Come on, Glory," Nolan says. "Slide onto Carter's cock, it will feel so good."

Fuck, these boys are dirty. I look around for Louis. He seems to be missing out. Louis comes to the side of the bed, carrying a bottle of lube, and my eyes widen in surprise. Carter turns my head back toward him as Louis climbs up on the bed on the other side. He leans in and kisses Carter, their tongues swirling. Carter pulls me closer and switches to me. Soon, we're close enough for all three of us to kiss. Pulling away, I straddle Carter and impale myself on his cock, gasping in shock. Even though Nolan has just fucked my brains out, Carter is a tight squeeze. I have to move up and down a couple of times before I am fully seated.

He pulls me in for a kiss, stroking my hair. "Such a good mate. Now relax."

Louis has moved down the bed behind me, and I feel a dribble of lube before he runs his finger around my tight hole. Carter thrusts upwards, distracting me. Moaning with pleasure, I start to ride him slowly. Nolan reaches down and circles a finger around my clit, then leans forward and sucks on a nipple, while Carter also leans forward and sucks on the other. They alternate between sucking, biting, and licking my nipples then kissing each other. Louis slowly slides one finger into my ass. I pause, tensing up, and Carter thrusts.

Nolan bites particularly hard and pulls my hair. "Pay attention, baby." His hand leaves my hair, and he starts to circle my clit with one finger.

Louis is up to two fingers now, and oh, it feels so good. I want to ride Carter faster, but he holds me still. Nolan stops circling my clit, and I whimper at the loss.

"No, I want more." I can feel my eyes start to glow as my gluttony demon comes to the forefront. "More. Now!" I demand.

Louis scissors three fingers in and out, the bite of pain providing a contrast to the pleasure the others are causing. "Okay, okay, greedy girl."

I get a slap on the ass before I feel the blunt head of his cock pushing in.

"Whoa." My eyes widen in shock.

The other two start up again, licking and biting my tits, and Nolan's finger circles my clit. I start to ramp up again, panting and gasping. Finally, he is fully seated, and I am stuffed full of cock.

Louis leans forward and kisses Carter. "I can feel you, *mon amour*."

I lean in a little and join the kiss. I really like these three-way kisses. So sexy. Louis's and Carter's hands both reach for my hips.

"Ready, *ma belle*?" Louis asks me.

Unable to respond due to the feelings running through my body, I just nod, and with that, Carter and Louis alternate between thrusting and retreating. A fiery blaze of passion rampages through my body. Grunts and groans fill the air, and the smell of sex and sweat hit my nose, ramping up the sensations. The burning blaze crests to a peak, then it all happens at once. Nolan pinches my clit, Carter bites my nipple, and Louis smacks my ass, and my body explodes.

Crying out, I sob my way through my orgasm, riding the wave of pleasure as it burns through my veins. My body shudders before finally surrendering, and Louis and Carter thrust twice more before groaning in unison as they fill me with their cum.

"That's two," Carter whispers in my ear, his breath ragged, "and we're just getting started."

I shiver from his words and feel a double click as both their mate bonds snap into place. Smiling with smug contentment, I watch as Nolan, who has been fisting his cock with his other hand, pumps once, and a rope of cum shoots onto his stomach. Leaning forward, I lick it all up, running my tongue over his rigid abdomen. Once I finish, I sit up. Louis has pulled out and is lying next to Carter. I admire my three men before I acknowledge their looks of shock, and then I wink at them.

"What? I can't let good food go to waste!" Climbing off Carter, I stretch languidly then snuggle in next to them. "A girl could get used to eating so well."

Chapter Eleven

All four of us lie there, enjoying the feeling as our bonds swirl into place. My head rests on Carter's chest, and his heartbeat thuds in my ear. It's beating in sync with mine, and I'm sure if I reached over and felt their pulses, Nolan's and Louis's would be the same.

Nolan stretches, a groan slipping out, and then he grunts as he rolls over, placing a kiss on each of us. "I need a shower. I have to pick up the girls soon." Sliding off the bed, he walks into the bathroom and turns the shower on. I can't say I'm sad to see him go, because his ass is a work of art.

"I must get ready too. I need to go to the restaurant and do some orders," Louis says. His French accent is husky and low as he, too, gives Carter and I both a kiss. I watch as he also walks to the bathroom, thanking my lucky stars for the gloriousness of my mates.

He joins Nolan in the shower. I can see them through the open door, and I watch as he pulls him close. They kiss deeply, their hands exploring each other's bodies. I rub my legs together to try and ease the ache that's starting to build again at the erotic sight.

A low chuckle from behind has me looking up into Carter's eyes. "Do you like what you see, cupcake?" He turns my head back toward the door to the bathroom then pushes me up and onto my hands and knees before leaning over me, caging me in place. I watch as Louis drops to his knees and takes Nolan's cock into his mouth. Nolan braces his hands against the shower wall and closes his eyes, his head tipping back in pleasure.

"Do you like seeing Louis down on his knees?" he whispers in my ear as his hands roam my body. He massages the glorious aches and pains they created, causing me to groan in relief and arousal.

Nolan flexes his hips, moving his cock deeper, and Louis's hands fondle his balls before I watch him slip a finger into his ass. Nolan thrusts harder and grunts in pleasure. God, the sight is sexy. My nipples are tight peaks, and I wiggle on my hands and knees as Carter continues to caress me, hoping his hands will drift to where I need them.

"What's wrong, baby? Do you have another ache that needs to be eased?" he whispers in my ear before placing kisses down my spine. I can feel the cum from before dripping down my leg as my core throbs in anticipation.

With one hand gripping my hip, he thrusts into me to the hilt. A moan escapes my mouth at the same time a deep, guttural groan leaves Nolan's as he stops his thrusts. I watch Louis's throat work as he swallows him down. Panting breaths escape my mouth as Carter works me over with lazy, languid strokes.

He leans down and says, "Keep watching," so I do. Louis, having finished swallowing, stands up and brings Nolan in for a kiss before turning him around and bending him over slightly. His hands follow the contours of Nolan's body until he reaches his hips. I see him grab a bottle and squeeze what must be lubricant onto his hand, and then he coats his cock with it. Grabbing the base of his dick, he lines up with Nolan's ass and thrusts deep. Both grunt in pleasure before Louis starts the same lazy, languid strokes that Carter is using on me. I can hear him talking in French as he thrusts, and although I don't understand, it brings my desire to a new level.

Carter reaches around and tweaks a nipple, the bite of pain exquisite as I watch Louis grab Nolan's quickly recovering cock. He thrusts and strokes in sync. The muscles in my legs are protesting the prolonged position, but nothing could stop me from what we're doing.

Carter's hand leaves my abused nipple to travel down to my clit. The sensations of touch and sound, combined with what I'm watching, is too much. With a delicate slide of his finger across my clit, I detonate like an atomic bomb. White light clouds my vision as pure pleasure flows through my body.

I collapse to the mattress, unable to hold myself up with my spaghetti arms. Carter keeps a vicious grip on my hips, which I know will leave marks tomorrow, but his thrusts prolong my orgasm, so I can't bring myself to care. He thrusts a few more times, and then he growls as his orgasm hits him.

Looking up, I watch as Louis pounds hard into Nolan before he shouts loudly in French and stills his hips while he continues to stroke Nolan's cock. Nolan also shouts, painting the shower wall with ropes of his cum. Louis relaxes against Nolan, and I watch as Nolan turns his head and they exchange kisses.

Carter pulls out and collapses next to me, wrapping his arms around me. With his eyes closed, and breath still heaving in and out, he whispers, "That's three."

A smile crosses my face, and I snuggle into his chest as darkness claims me.

*

Sometime later, I wake to a warm, cozy feeling surrounding my body. Opening my eyes, I find Carter's arms wrapped around me. I'm the little spoon to his big spoon. I feel the urgent need to pee, so I slowly shimmy out of his embrace and move to the bathroom. He grumbles and grabs hold of my pillow in his sleep, pulling it closer and holding on tight. A warm feeling inside my chest brings a smile to my lips. Who would have thought that I would end up with three mates? Serena is never going to believe me. I need to give her a call and fill her in.

Once I finish using the bathroom, I give my tousled hair a brush and wrap a robe around my naked body. It's a men's robe that's way too big for me, but I pull the belt tight, and it holds. Sneaking past Carter, I head for the kitchen.

Now that the latent lusty side of me has been taken care of, the gluttony side roars to life, and although my energy has been a lot more stable since the bonds clicked into place, all that sex has worked up an appetite.

As I make my way downstairs, I realize the house is quiet. Nolan hasn't returned from picking up the girls yet, and Louis must still be at the restaurant. The clock in the kitchen tells me it's mid-afternoon. Opening the fridge, I peer in and take stock of what they have to offer. Before I can get far, a knock at the front door draws my attention. Grabbing an apple, I close the fridge and head toward the sound, and when the persistent knocking continues, I open it.

Taking a bite of my apple, I survey the two people standing there. The man is dressed in a suit and has a briefcase at his feet. His hair is combed to the side and gelled to within an inch of its life. He has square-rimmed glasses, and his eyes look cold and unforgiving. The woman has a haughty look on her face and is dressed in a severe skirt suit. She's tall and slim with dark tousled hair. She would fit perfectly with the bitches from the wedding yesterday.

I let them wait while I finish my mouthful of apple. After swallowing, I ask, "May I help you?"

The man hands me his business card and says, "My name is Jackson Jones, and I am a partner at Schwimmer, Shuester, and Jones. I represent Miss Bridgette Blake." He gestures to the woman next to him.

Raising my eyebrows, I take the card and look it over. "Okay, cool, but I'm not quite sure who Miss Bridgette Blake is," I tell him.

A frown creases both of their faces. "Where's Nolan?" the haughty woman demands, trying to look around me. I stand my ground and pull the door slightly closed, not allowing her to look.

"Not here at the moment. Can I give him a message? Or better yet, how about you call and make an appointment before you just rock up at his house?" I suggest with ice in my voice, not liking the tone she's using. I start to close the door, but the lawyer sticks his foot in the frame before I can close it. I'm prepared to zap him with my magic when his next words stop me dead.

"We have been ordered to look into the living arrangements of Mr. Nolan Stephens. The court is worried that Miss Zoe and Aria Stephens are living in some less than ideal living conditions, and their mother, Miss Blake, has requested that it is assessed so she can gain sole custody."

My stomach sinks, and I open the door wide again, shooting the gloating woman a dirty look. "You had better come in then. He won't be long, he's just out picking the girls up from their friend's place." I hold the door open, and the couple enters. I show them into the living area and gesture to the large sectional. "Please have a seat. I'm just going to get dressed."

Before they can say anything else, I turn and race back upstairs, launching myself at Carter's body, shaking him hard.

"Carter, wake up," I whisper. Without waiting for him to answer, I run around, looking for something to wear. Luckily, I see my bags in the corner of the room. I pull out some jeans and a T-shirt and quickly throw on some underwear. "Carter, fucking wake up," I hiss louder, and he peers at me somewhat dazed. "There's a woman downstairs claiming to be the girls' mom, and she has a lawyer."

That gets a reaction. He bolts straight out of bed. I take a moment to admire his physique—hey, a girl has needs—before running into the bathroom, picking up his clothes, and throwing them at him.

"What's the plan? How are we playing this?" My words tumble out, sounding breathless as my worry increases. "They say they've heard rumors of unsuitable living conditions. Humans are so judgy. They are not going to understand me being with all of you. They are just going to make up dirty lies." Tears start to gather in my eyes.

Carter finishes dressing and pulls me close, pressing a gentle kiss to my forehead. "Take a deep breath, Glory, and slow down. It will be fine. For the sake of the humans, you'll be Nolan's fiancée. It's no one else's business that Louis and I live here too." He goes over to the bedside table and pulls out a box. Opening it, he shows me a ring nestled in red velvet.

A gasp leaves my mouth as he pulls it out and grabs my left hand.

"I'm sure Nolan and Louis will forgive me for this given the circumstances, but this was Nolan's grandmother's ring. She gave it to him and told him to give it to his mate. That's you." He slides the beautiful ring onto my finger.

I admire the stunning piece of jewelry. Shaped like a sunflower, the center stone is a beautiful green gem surrounded by white stones, acting as the petals of the ring.

"The center is alexandrite, thought to bring luck, good fortune, and love. Nolan's grandmother is Russian, and she says alexandrite is a good omen. The outside gems are diamonds." He pulls me close and places a gentle kiss on my lips before pulling away and saying, "Right, let's go deal with that devil spawn." He pulls me by the hand, and we head downstairs and into the kitchen, bypassing the living area.

I frown at Carter when he helps me onto a stool in the kitchen and proceeds to put the coffee machine on. The island is still covered in all the different macarons. "What are you doing?" I ask him in confusion. "They are waiting on the couch."

He looks up and winks at me. "I thought you would like to sample some of the macarons that Louis and the girls made you."

I smile at his thoughtfulness and reach for one.

"Besides, there's nothing that drives Bridgette crazier than being ignored. Just you wait," he predicts.

"Know her well, do you?" I ask as the little green jealousy monster rears its ugly head. Funny, isn't it? This man boned my sister five ways to Sunday two days prior, and I didn't even blink, but now that he's my mate, the claws come out.

He laughs at my tone and comes around and gives me a hug. "Oh, baby, you have nothing to worry about. Even when my energy was at its lowest, I wouldn't have touched her. That's why I used your sister's agency. Bridgette was the mother of Nolan's children, and I wasn't touching that with a ten-foot pole, though she did try a few times."

He goes back around to the other side of the bench and finishes making coffee. Before he can pass me my cup, a throat clearing sound can be heard coming from the doorway into the living area. I look up, and Bridgette is standing there with her arms crossed and toes tapping.

"We're waiting!" she announces loudly.

"We know! Nolan should be home any minute," Carter replies, sitting down next to me.

An exasperated sigh leaves her mouth. "Aren't you going to offer us anything to drink?"

Carter turns to face her. "No. You were not invited, and you arrived unannounced. Now, if you had gone about it the right way and called beforehand, then maybe." He shrugs, turns back around, and proceeds to drink his coffee.

I watch, hiding a smile behind my cup, as she flounces back to the living room. Leaning over, I place a kiss on his cheek. "Good job."

Chapter Twelve

Carter and I sit there for about thirty minutes, drinking coffee and eating macarons while we talk quietly and get to know each other better. He gets up a couple of times to make sure that the lawyer and Nolan's ex aren't wandering around the house snooping, but we feel no need to entertain them when they arrived so rudely unannounced.

Carter is just getting up to check on them again when we hear the sound of gravel crunching as Nolan drives up the driveway. We both leave the kitchen and make our way into the living area where Bridgette and her lawyer are still waiting.

She has an annoyed look on her face. "Finally," she snaps, standing up. "I am paying by the hour, you know."

Carter just walks past her, opening the front door for Nolan and the girls.

They all walk in, the girls chattering excitedly as they tell their dad about their day. They stop abruptly at the sight of Bridgette. Nolan and Aria adopt almost identical scowls, but Zoe looks past her to me and shouts, "Mommy!"

She runs toward me, her arms wide open. In shock, I open mine and crouch down to receive the bundle of energy.

She throws her little arms around me and hugs me tight as she whispers, "Daddy says you're going to marry him, and you're going to be my mommy from now on."

My heart skips a beat in delight, and I hug her tighter, whispering back, "I would love to be your mommy."

When I look up at Nolan in surprise, he shrugs his shoulders and smiles before turning back to Bridgette. Standing up, I lift Zoe into my arms and look at Bridgette too. The shock and then fury that crosses her face would be scary if I wasn't a demon and absolutely not afraid of her.

"What the hell, Nolan? Who is this woman, and why wasn't I informed of the changes?" She gestures toward me angrily.

Nolan just scoffs and shakes his head before turning to Carter. "Can you get our lawyer on the phone, please?"

Carter nods and leaves the room to make the call.

Bridgette's lawyer steps forward and hands Nolan another card. Nolan doesn't even look at it, he just brushes past the two of them and comes over to give me a gentle kiss on the lips. His eyes gleam when he catches sight of the ring on my finger. Aria follows closely behind him, making a considerable detour past her mother. Bridgette doesn't even try to talk to her, her focus entirely on Nolan.

"Mr. Stephens, we have had some disturbing reports regarding the girls' living arrangements and have a court order to have the household investigated. We were not aware that another woman was living in the house. We had been informed that it's three men, and that you all have questionable relationships with each other. The court order says that the girls are to be taken into custody by child protective services until the matter has been resolved."

A look of fury crosses Nolan's face. Aria steps closer to me and reaches up to grab one of my hands, and tears start to brim in her eyes as her bottom lip quivers. I don't think Zoe quite understands, but she can see how upset her dad and sister are, and her little arms tighten around my neck.

"Now, just a minute. I'm not sure where you got your information from, but this is my fiancée, and she has only just moved in. As for the rest of your information, where did that come from? Was it a reliable source?" he questions the lawyer before turning to Aria. "Can you take Zoe upstairs, please? Find Uncle Carter, and he will put something on the television for you to watch."

Zoe clings to me, but I give her a kiss and put her down, whispering for her to go with Aria. I tell her I'll come and find them shortly. Nodding, she lets Aria take her hand, and they leave. Once he's assured of their distance, Nolan turns his wrath on Bridgette.

"As for you, I have signed papers saying you waived all rights to your children for a sum of money. Do you really think that says mother of the year? Do you think they will award a woman like that custody of children she clearly doesn't value over money? I don't have to inform you of any changes because you signed your rights away and haven't looked back once. Zoe didn't even recognize you." The fierceness in his voice has her stepping back.

I walk over and grab his hand, lending my silent support. It's taking everything in me not to set them both on fire.

The lawyer opens his briefcase and pulls out a sheet of paper. "Well, we actually have a letter signed by a psychiatrist that says she had post-partum depression and wasn't in her right mind to be signing away her rights to her children."

A smug grin crosses her face as Nolan's hand tightens in mine.

"No one has informed me or my representation of any changes, and they will not be going anywhere with you until my lawyer has assessed all the relevant information and spoken to the presiding judge." He's so angry, I can feel him vibrating.

Wanting to avoid any kind of bloodshed or the

chance of breaking a nail while burying a couple of bodies, I step forward and open the door. "Please leave, and next time you decide to visit, make a phone call, preferably to his lawyer first," I tell them, gesturing for them to leave. Just to stick it to the manipulative bitch, I add, "You're not welcome in my house, and you're most definitely not welcome to my children."

Her face turns red, and she raises her hand to slap me. *Oh yes. Bring it, bitch, I can claim self-defense.* Unfortunately, the lawyer grabs her and drags her out without any more words.

Closing the door behind them, I turn to Nolan who now has an amused look on his face and his eyebrows raised.

"What?" I ask. "It is my house, and they are my children." I wave my engagement ring at him. "This says so. You liked it, so you put a ring on it, or Carter did anyway. You're stuck with me now, or so says Queen B."

A wicked smile crosses his lips, and he stalks toward me with a gleam in his eye. I back up until he pins me against the front door. Caging me with his forearms, he leans in, and his scent tickles my nose.

His breath caresses my ear as he whispers, "Oh, baby, there's no getting away now." He claims my mouth with a possessive kiss.

I melt against him, dragging him closer, and sigh with contentment.

He pulls back and rests his forehead against mine, then he lifts my left hand to his mouth and places a kiss on my ring finger. "I do like seeing our ring on your hand."

We just stand there, breathing it all in, but subconsciously, we know shit's about to hit the fan. The handle tries to turn, dragging us both out of our musings. We step away from the door and Louis walks in, a frown on his face.

"Was that Bridgette I saw driving away?" he asks, gesturing outside. "What was she doing here?"

A smile crosses my face. He is so adorable with his French accent and his confused expression. I move away from Nolan and wrap my arms around Louis, hugging him tight. I need all the contact I can get from our little family, because my worry is at an all-time high.

The frown leaves his face, and he smiles softly at me, placing a gentle kiss on my lips. "Hello, my little eclair, I have missed you."

Nolan blows out a frustrated breath, running both hands through his hair before shouting, "Carter, get down here!"

We all move over to the sofas. Louis and I are in one, his arm wrapped around me as he absently plays with the ring on my finger, and Nolan collapses into the other, his face covered in worry. Carter's feet are loud as he runs down the stairs before joining Nolan on the opposite sofa, throwing an arm behind him and giving him a comforting squeeze.

"The girls are watching a movie, and The Brad is on his way," Carter tells Nolan before turning to me. "The Brad is our lawyer."

I nod my head, slightly confused over the name, but okay.

"Yes, it was Bridgette. She's making a play for the girls," Nolan tells Louis, his tone despondent. "I didn't think there would be any way she could after she signed away her rights, but postpartum depression just might win it for her."

Carter pulls him closer. "Look, let's not worry about it until The Brad gets here. He will have answers for us."

I sit up, pulling away from Louis. "You trust something as important as this to someone who calls himself The Brad?" I ask incredulously.

They all share a laugh, and Carter explains, "Bradley Smythe III went to school with us, and when we were freshmen, he decided he wanted to be known as The Brad. He thought it would be cool or something. He eventually outgrew it, but the name stuck for some of us. It's a running joke. He's a wrath demon and very, very good at what he does. He'll have some answers for us."

"Well, what should we do while we wait?" I ask.

All three men look at me with heat in their eyes and smirks on their faces.

"Not that," I scold them. "The girls are upstairs."

Louis stands up and stretches. "Well, if we can't do that, then I will make us a celebratory dinner." He winks at me. "It's not every day a girl gets engaged."

Nolan looks a little sad. "I'm sorry, Glory. Not that it happened, but about the way it happened. We would have made it special for you."

The other two nod their heads.

I glance down at the ring on my finger and look up at my mates. "I'm not sorry at all. I don't need romance and candles. I'm so happy to have you. I'm just sad that I can't marry all three of you." I notice now that they all wear matching rings—black circles with a band of gold through the middle. "What's that?" I ask, pointing to them.

Louis answers, "When Nolan escaped Bridgette, we decided we wanted to make a commitment to each other, even though we knew we would possibly meet mates. We never dreamed we would share one and that we would also share mating marks with each other. It was more a symbol of our friendship and how it would never get broken."

I smile at the answer. "I want a ring like that too, please."

Louis grabs one of my hands and yanks me off the couch and into his arms. "For you, my little dumpling, anything." He twirls me around.

Giggles erupt from me at his silly behavior, and

he smacks a kiss on my lips before putting me down and wandering off toward the kitchen. Watching him go is no hardship. A tug on the hand disturbs my admiration as Carter pulls me down onto the sofa with him and Nolan. My ass is in his lap while my legs are draped over Nolan's.

"He cooks when he's worried," Nolan tells me. "It will keep him occupied until The Brad gets here. Now, what should we do to keep ourselves busy, beautiful?"

Carter places little kisses on my shoulder as Nolan runs his hands up my legs, the gentle motions pulling a quiet moan from my lips, but the sound of feet on the stairs interrupts us as two nosy little girls come running from upstairs. I try to escape the two men, but they hold firm, though their attention is now on the little girls.

"Are we having a cuddle pile with Mommy?" Zoe asks, throwing herself onto us.

A whoosh of breath escapes my lungs as an elbow connects with my belly, but the feeling of pure joy soaring through me at her innocence and acceptance negates any pain. Aria stands close by but seems a little more hesitant until I hold out my hand, pulling her into the pile. Her high-pitched giggles shortly join Zoe's as Nolan and Carter tickle us all. It's a much needed distraction from the tension surrounding us.

Pulling back, I tell the girls, "There are still a lot of macarons left over from this morning. If you hurry, I'm sure you can catch Uncle Louis before he puts them all away. Maybe you can grab a couple."

They both jump off the couch, and Zoe races toward the kitchen. Aria follows, but she stops, turns around, and shyly says, "Are you coming too, Mom?"

I nod my head in shock, and she smiles before following Zoe. Stunned and so very pleased, I feel tears of joy stream down my face as I look at both Carter and Nolan.

"She called me Mom. I didn't think she would want to."

Nolan wipes the tears from my cheeks as Carter pulls me in, hugging me tight.

"Bridgette never wanted to be called Mom, said she was too young and insisted that Aria call her by her name," Nolan says. "Although not as obvious as Zoe, she's thrilled you're joining our family."

I sigh with delight and give them both a kiss before moving out of their laps and following after the girls. *My girls.* Life is good.

Chapter Thirteen

Sometime later, Louis has dinner bubbling on the stove, and the girls and I are splashing around in the pool while the guys meet with The Brad. Much to my relief, he arrives in a Porsche, and he's wearing an expensive suit and carrying a briefcase. I envisioned Hawaiian shirts and flip-flops, so to say I was reassured is an understatement. I desperately wanted to be involved in the conversation, but Nolan asked me to keep the girls company and said he would fill me in later. There was no way I was going to argue with him.

Climbing out, I dry myself off and lie down on a sun lounger to watch the girls. The monster dog—who I've discovered belongs to Carter—is named Max, and he makes himself comfortable on the ground next to me. His tongue hangs out of his mouth, and he pants after spending some time running around the pool, jumping in and out, and barking at the girls. Aria is patiently helping Zoe swim around the shallow end with a pool noodle, while Zoe chatters away without a care in the world.

"Mommy." My heart jumps in joy every time she says it. "Can you ask Daddy for a baby, please?"

I sit up in surprise as she goes on.

"We want a little brother. Don't we, Aria?" She looks to her for confirmation, and Aria screws up her nose.

My heart drops. Maybe she doesn't want another child in the family.

"Not a brother, boys are smelly. A sister, please." And just like that, she puts in her request and eases my worries.

I lie back down, my hand going over my belly. I guess there's a chance there could already be one on the way. It's not like we used protection. "I'll let Daddy know your requests," I tell them both. *And Uncle Louis and Uncle Carter.* So much has happened since yesterday. I really can't believe it. I have to call Serena and let her know I'm okay, since the last time she saw me I was threatening bodily harm.

I conjure my phone, and it appears in my hand. I dial Serena's number, but it rings out and goes to her messages. I wait for the beep and leave one.

"Hey, sis, give me a call when you get a chance. I have so much to tell you." Pressing the screen, I hang up and return my phone to where it came from. I stretch my arms and decide it's time to get the girls out of the pool and feed them some dinner. It's getting late, and the meeting with The Brad is taking longer than I thought.

*A*fter dinner and a bath, I read the girls a story. *Hansel and Gretel* is the request. I'm surprised, thinking it might be too scary, but the girls just laugh at me. We finish up, and after lots of cuddles, I turn out the lights and pull the door almost closed on the girls' room, leaving a crack for the hallway light to shine through.

I make my way back downstairs to see what the guys are up to. The Brad was just leaving when the girls said goodnight to the guys, and I want to know what was discussed. I find them sitting in the lounge, all with a beer in hand. They look a lot more relaxed than I thought they would, and my worries ease slightly.

I throw myself onto the couch next to Louis and snuggle in. Grabbing his beer, I take a sip before handing it back. He smirks before taking another sip himself.

"So who's going to tell me what happened?" I ask when they remain quiet.

Nolan's face is calm, but his hair looks like he's been running his hand through it continuously, while Carter seems as cool as a cucumber, as always.

"The Brad did some digging," Nolan begins. "It looks like Bridgette has burned through all the money I gave her for the girls. The lawyer is her new boyfriend, and the psychiatrist is his uncle.

They couldn't provide any proof on the supposed source of information. The court order was legit, but when Brad called the judge and explained the circumstances, he withdrew his support and canceled the investigation into our home, especially after he heard about my fiancée." He winks at me, and I blow him a kiss. "Child services also hadn't ordered for the children to be taken. They were just going to do some in-home visits to assess the situation. Brad has now filed a restraining order against both Bridgette and the lawyer. Hopefully, that will be the end of it."

A huge weight lifts off my chest at Nolan's words. Our family is safe. My stomach rumbles loudly, breaking the tension, and the guys all laugh.

"Why don't we all sit down and eat the dinner Louis prepared? Better late than never, right?" I suggest to the guys. I didn't eat when the girls did, and now I'm starving. "I saw a bottle of bubbly sitting in the fridge when I looked before."

Carter stands and offers me his hand. Grabbing hold, I let him pull me up from the couch, and then he wraps an arm around me and leads me to the kitchen.

"What a great idea. Then, when we're done, I believe I still owe you something."

My core clenches at the thought, and I nod my head in agreement. "Oh yes, you most definitely do."

Dinner is a pleasant affair. It's the first chance

we've had to sit down and get to know each other better, so it's a long, drawn-out process with mouth-watering food and delicious wine and champagne. I learned that the three guys are business partners, and Tasty Treats is not the only business they run. They also own a nightclub and a bail bonds agency. Nolan is a bounty hunter, and Louis and Carter help out if he needs them.

I bounce up and down on my seat at this news. A bounty hunter? I would be an excellent bounty hunter. "Oh, oh, please can I join the agency? I would make an awesome bounty hunter." Standing up, I make a gun with my hands, Charlie's Angels style, and point it at Nolan. "Freeze, motherfucker."

The guys dissolve into fits of laughter, and Carter just about falls off his chair.

A frown crosses my face, and I sit back down, disappointed. "Assholes," I mutter under my breath. "I'm going to get a taser and fry your asses."

This just causes more laughter. Crossing my arms, I roll my eyes at them.

Nolan composes himself, gets up, and walks toward me. "Honey, if that's what you would like to do, then I can take you to the range. You need to be licensed to carry a gun first. Let's see how you do with that. There's no point in getting ahead of ourselves." He pulls me up and tugs me close, giving me a kiss on the forehead. "I'm sure you would be an awesome bounty hunter."

Carter also gets up and comes over, pulling us

both close. "You'd certainly be a sexy distraction," he says, placing kisses on both our lips.

My core throbs again at the sight of Carter and Nolan kissing. Watching these men show affection for each other is so sexy.

Louis joins us, making our circle complete. "You would be a *magnifique* bounty hunter, I'm sure, but what about your blog? Wouldn't you miss your food?"

I just shake my head at him and smile. "Couldn't I do both? You all help each other out. I want to contribute to our family."

He smiles at me. "If that is what you want, my little dumpling, but you being here with us and being a mother to the girls is plenty enough. Why don't you take a few days to think about it?"

My lip pouts a little more. I know I'm being childish, but they may be surprised at what I know.

Nolan looks at me knowingly. "I'll still take you to the range if you want."

A smile crosses my face, and I nod enthusiastically. The guys all laugh again, and Nolan and Louis step away to clear the table.

Carter smacks my ass, and I yelp, rubbing away the sting. He starts toward the stairs. "Come on. While they are clearing the table and cleaning up, I'll run you a bath, princess."

I look toward the guys to see if they need help, but Louis just shoos me away.

Chasing after Carter, I head toward the master

bedroom where we all were before. At dinner, they told me that this was now our room, although Louis and Carter would keep theirs for the time being. We need to have a conversation with the girls about the actual status of our relationship. I refuse to hide what we are to each other, and I want to be able to kiss or show affection to each of the guys without hesitation, especially in our own home. I also want to go to sleep in their arms every night and wake up to their faces every morning.

The door is wide open when I arrive, and I can hear water running into the swimming pool they call a tub in the adjoining bathroom. Recessed into the ground, it's almost large enough to swim laps in. When I get there, Carter is sprinkling bath salts into it, and the scent of jasmine and vanilla surrounds me as steam fills the room.

"Come on, baby, strip and climb in. I'll go get you another glass of wine to have while you're relaxing." He strides out, placing a gentle kiss on my lips as he goes, and I feel a little disappointed. I thought he would want to join me. It must show on my face, because he gives me a wink. "I'll be right back. Make sure you leave some room for me."

He leaves, and I strip before stepping down into the steaming hot water. The day's tension drains away as I find a seat and lay my head back, closing my eyes. I can't believe how much has happened in such a short period of time. Mom always said it was a whirlwind of a ride when you met your mate. Boy, is she going to be surprised when I tell her this story.

Peaceful, soothing music starts to play. Opening my eyes, I find speakers set into the walls and see that Carter has returned. He sets two glasses of champagne down on the floor next to the bath, and I watch as he removes his clothes. He strips off his shirt, his muscles rippling with the movement. The man is built like a god. Unbuckling his jeans, he lets them drop to the floor, revealing his thick, erect cock. It truly is a mouthwatering sight.

He joins me in the water, passing a glass of champagne to me before grabbing one for himself. "To us." Carter clinks his glass against mine.

I take a sip, the bubbles tickling my tongue. He doesn't take a drink, instead grabbing me by the waist with his other hand and dragging me onto his lap. I straddle him, his cock pushing against my stomach, my breasts now above the water.

He takes his glass of champagne and pours some of it across my chest before suckling the liquid from my skin. Carter runs his tongue around one of my nipples before drawing it into his mouth and sucking hard. The sensation shoots straight to my clit, causing it to throb, and he alternates between the two until his glass is empty. By the time he's finished, I'm squirming on his lap, needing to feel him inside me.

"Please, Carter." I'm panting with want.

Putting his glass to the side, he grips my hips.

"What is it, baby? Tell me what you want." His mouth slides along my jawline to my ear, where he nibbles and places tiny kisses.

"Fuck me, please."

His mouth slams onto mine, hot and heavy, and his tongue thrusts like I want his cock to. I reach up and grab hold of his hair, pulling it, and he grunts into my mouth before lifting me slightly and thrusting up into my clenching pussy. A moan escapes my lips as the feeling of fullness throbs through my body. Pulling back, he looks into my eyes as he moves me up and down in a slow, sensual glide. Love shines in his eyes as the intensity builds.

His hands caress up and down my back before gripping my hips harder. His movements speed up, and the water starts to slosh over the side of the tub. Animalistic sounds escape our mouths as the slow burn turns scorching, and then his hand slides down between us.

Pulling his mouth away from mine, he rasps, "Come for me, baby," and pinches my clit.

An exquisite explosion flows through my body. I throw my head back, and my groan of pleasure echoes around the bathroom. I feel my pussy clench on his cock as he thrusts through my orgasm before he, too, fills the bathroom with his groans. His eyes are closed, and he is biting his lip. His pleasure is so sexy, and his throbbing cock extends my orgasm. Slowly, our breathing settles, and I snuggle into him. His cock is still in me, and I can feel it softening slightly, but I don't care. The intimacy of the moment makes me want to stay here forever.

"That's four," he whispers a short time later, and a smile crosses my lips. Pulling back, he shoots me a mischievous grin, and my breath hitches. This man is in my heart. They all are.

I climb off him, and we wash and get out. Thick, warm towels are waiting for us, as are our other two men. Louis and Nolan hold out the towels for us. After quickly drying off, we join them in bed. They put me in the middle, surrounding me on all sides. I feel content and relaxed. Kisses are exchanged, and my eyes close as I hear them tell me they love me.

Chapter Fourteen

The next morning, we have breakfast as a family. The girls' excited chatter fills the kitchen, as does the smell of cooking bacon. The island is packed high with waffles and pancakes with an assortment of syrups and toppings to go with them. Louis, wearing an apron with a cartoon chef on it, stands at the stove and expertly flips more pancakes. Nolan and Carter are both dressed in cargo pants with tight black shirts with Wrathful Bail Bonds written on them. They are both needed on a job today, so I'm in charge of the girls. I've decided to take them to a nearby park to run off some energy.

"Mommy, will you push me on the swings?" Zoe asks me hopefully.

Taking a sip of my coffee, I nod my head. "Of course I will."

She looks pleased but a little worried. "Not too high, though, okay?"

Smothering a smile, I agree not to push her too high.

The girls finish eating, and I send them upstairs to brush their teeth and put on their shoes. Nolan and Carter finish and put their plates in the dishwasher before coming over and giving me a kiss on the lips.

"Be safe," I tell them.

They wave goodbye and walk out the door, leaving me alone with Louis.

He puts down the bowl he was drying and walks toward me, swinging me around on the stool so I'm facing him and he has me caged in. Leaning down, he places a slow, sensual kiss on my lips. "Mmm, now that's what I call a good morning, my little love muffin."

I giggle at his nickname.

A gasp at the door has me looking up. Aria and Zoe are standing there with frowns on their faces. My heart starts to pound, and panic creeps in. Shit. We haven't talked to them about the situation yet, but the only thing that comes out of Aria's mouth is, "Did Daddy and Uncle Carter leave without saying goodbye?"

I look at Louis in surprise. "Nolan, Carter, and I had a chat with the girls before you got up this morning. They know what's going on and that it's nobody's business but ours."

I turn to answer Aria's question, but Zoe has moved on. "Daddy told us that our new brother is going to have three daddies and one mommy and that you all love each other and us very much."

Well, okay then, I guess that's that.

My heart starts to calm, and Louis gives the girls

each a kiss on the cheek before handing me a back-pack. "I've packed some snacks and drinks for your trip. I need to go into the restaurant for a little while today. I have a few staffing issues to sort out."

I start to feel guilty, and it must show on my face, because he shakes his head at me.

"No, Glory, don't do that. None of it was your fault. They truly deserved what they got." With that, he grabs a set of keys off the island and hands them to me. "Nolan left his car with the girls' seats in it for you. We'll have to organize to pick yours up from your old place, as well as anything else you need, sometime soon."

I take them from him, and then he gives me another quick kiss and waves goodbye before running upstairs to get changed.

Zoe grabs my hand and drags me out to the garage. "Come on, Mommy, we need to go before the park gets too busy and all the other kids steal the swings."

Aria rolls her eyes but hurries after us as well.

Pulling into a space by the park, I help the girls out of their seats before we make our way over to a shady area. While they remove their shoes, I take out a picnic blanket and place it on the ground, then I throw the backpack Louis packed us on top.

The park is deserted, but it's still very early, so it really isn't a surprise. I head over to the girls at the swing set and start pushing them on the swings. We've been in the park for about half an hour before we see signs of other people. The girls climb up to the top of the slide and whizz down at high speed, while I wait at the bottom to catch them, their giggles filling the park with joy and laughter.

As I wait for them to climb, I see a black van with tinted windows pull into the parking lot. It drives very slowly before pulling into a spot next to mine. Just as I lose interest, I hear a loud crunching sound. Turning back, I see that the black van has hit Nolan's car. *Crap*.

I call to the girls, asking them to slide down, and they do so. I don't want to leave them up at the top while I deal with this.

I walk to the car to examine the damage. The bumper is crumpled in, but there doesn't seem to be any damage to the van. Both front doors open, and out climb two very similar-looking men—brothers, if I'm not mistaken—who have thick bodies and double chins. One has his black hair shaved close to his head, and the other man has his grown out, the long, greasy strands brushing his shoulders.

They come around to look down at the damage, and the one from the driver's side says, "Oops."

My anger starts to rise. "Oops? That's all you have to say?"

The girls have joined us now, their curiosity getting the better of them.

The driver is smug. "Well, yeah, but it got me what I needed."

I look between him and the passenger, and my

heart drops into my stomach as they both pull guns and point them at me. The girls whimper and move as close to me as they can.

"We don't want to hurt anyone. Be calm, and this will go smoothly. The girls need to get into the van." The passenger goes to the sliding door, opens it, and gestures with his gun for the girls to get in, but he must have pushed the clip release on his gun as he did so, because it falls to the ground with a clatter.

The stunned look on his face is hysterical. Laughter bubbles up in my throat before spilling out of my mouth. He scrambles to pick up the clip and shoves it back into the gun before pointing it at us again.

The driver rolls his eyes and mutters, "Fuck," before saying, "Shut up, bitch. Tell the children to get in the car, and we'll let you go."

I snap my head around to the man who's talking to me. I feel my eyes change color, and the wrath part of me that comes from Nolan creeps to the front. I pull the girls close, wrapping my arms around them.

"Not a fucking chance, buddy."

A shocked look crosses his face, and he shakes his head before looking toward the other gunman, who shrugs his shoulders. They both seem a little bewildered by my reaction.

"What do you care? They are not your kids. Are they worth your life?" the long-haired man asks.

"Who told you they are not my children? They may not have come from my womb, but they are mine, and nobody is taking them from me," I snarl at him, and the driver growls in frustration.

"Fine, hurry up and get in before I start putting holes in one of you. I don't need all of you to ask for a ransom."

Zoe starts to cry, but Aria is being very brave and tugging on my hand.

"Come on, Mom, let's just do what they say," Aria suggests.

I nod my head and help the girls into the van.

As I start to climb in, the passenger stops me and holds out his hand. "Phone, and put the passcode in," he demands.

Grabbing it out of my pocket, I enter my passcode and hand it to him. He shoves me in, and I stumble, sprawling across the floor of the van. It smells like paint and grease, and my nose wrinkles as the girls huddle against me in their fright. He takes my phone and snaps a shot of us before typing something, and then he must hit the send button before he drops it to the ground and smashes it under his foot. Damn it, maybe these guys aren't as dumb as I thought, though I'm not sure whom he sent the message to. I don't have any of the guys' numbers on my phone yet, and I'm kicking myself for the oversight.

He pulls the door shut and climbs into the front. There's a wall between us and the cab, and the driver must already be seated because the van starts and we begin moving. It's stupid of them, really, not being able to watch us, but I'm not complaining.

Zoe is crying in huge, gulping sobs, and Aria's brave face has crumbled, her tears silently streaming down her face.

Pulling them close, I wrap my arms around them and kiss them both on the cheek. "Don't you worry. I'll get us out of this, and remember, your daddy is a big bad bounty hunter. These guys are not going to know what hit them."

Glancing around the back of the van, I look for something I can use as a weapon. They left me untied, which wasn't smart. There's a huge pile of junk stacked in the back. I'm not sure if they are hoarders or maybe junkyard collectors, but the range is certainly eclectic. There are some old paint cans stacked on a shelf, which isn't going to be helpful unless I can get the drop on one of them, but that still leaves the other. *Damn it.*

My anger starts to rise again, and my stomach rumbles. The stress is making me burn through my energy quicker. I had snacks in the bag, but the backpack is still sitting in the park on the picnic blanket. I give Zoe to Aria to hold, and then I continue to hunt for a weapon, searching through the junk in the back of the van. A toolbox supplies me with a screwdriver, so I shove it into my back pocket and pull my shirt over the top. It may come in handy. There's also a box cutter, and that goes into the other pocket of my jeans. I find a shovel, but it's not like I can hide that on my body, so I leave it where it is. Thank goodness they weren't really thinking clearly when they shoved us in here. Moving back to the girls, I settle down and pull them close.

Nolan must know we've been taken by now. How long will it be until he finds the abandoned car at the park? How are they going to find us from there? My heart starts to sink, but an idea from the story I read the girls last night crosses my mind. Moving over to the side of the van, I pull out the screwdriver and use it to jimmy open the only window as far as I can, then I start to throw things out of the window, leaving a trail for the guys to follow. The gunmen must not be paying attention to the side mirrors, thankfully, and I must look like a madwoman, because Zoe's sobs ease and a giggle escapes her mouth.

Moving away from the window, I wipe her face down. "Good girl, be brave for me now. Maybe the two of you can pass me things to throw."

A shaky smile crosses her face, and she and Aria start to hand me things. I pile them next to me to drop periodically out the window. Perhaps a cop car will drive past and see me throwing all the junk out. That would be a miracle.

I started with the biggest things I could fit out the window that would draw the most attention, but I'm now down to knickknacks. Out goes an old beer sign, a dashboard hula dancer, a bobblehead Einstein figure, some pewter cups, and a bunch of fake flowers. Aria passes me an item, and it's like nothing I've ever seen before. It's a long, clear cylinder with a plastic tube attached to one end running to a bulb. I pump the bulb a couple of times before it dawns on me. *Oh fuck! Gross!* It's quickly ditched out the window. Holy crap. Who carries a penis pump in the back of their van?

The next couple of items the girls pass over are some magazines with naked ladies on the front, which are also swiftly thrown out the window. I'm going to need to use hand sanitizer when we get rescued, and so will the girls. Luckily they are so busy concentrating on what to throw next, they don't pay too much attention to the pictures.

Before long, I'm down to throwing individual tools out—a definite trail of breadcrumbs for the guys to follow. *How much farther do we have to go?* As I think this, the van slows and turns a corner. Panicking, I open one of the paint cans and pour it out the window, hoping it leaves enough of a mark for them to know we turned.

I peer out the window and see we are in a wooded area. From the feel of it, the road is gravel. Zoe and Aria get bumped around, so I abandon my task and pull them close to secure them so they don't get hurt. I make the decision then and there that I am going to do everything demonly possible to get these two beautiful children, who have welcomed and embraced me into their lives, back to their dad. I want to tell them to run for the forest and hide, but they are just too young, so it's up to me to keep them safe.

"Okay, listen up, girls."

Their big eyes are wide with fright, but they seem to be over their initial panic.

"I need you to stay behind me when we stop. No matter what happens, do everything the bad men say, please. I need you to be safe. If we can get away, we will."

They both nod their heads as the van comes to a stop.

<h1 style="text-align:center">Chapter Fifteen</h1>

As the van stops, I quickly open another can of paint and move closer to the door. Hopefully, the kidnappers will both be standing there when it opens.

The front doors slam, sounding like gunshots to me, as I wait for them to come let us out. It feels like forever. Anticipation wraps its hands around my throat and squeezes, my pulse racing as I wait. The door handle sounds like thunder, and the sliding of the door is like nails on a chalkboard to my heightened senses. Finally, it opens all the way, exposing the greasy, gun-toting kidnappers to my wrath.

With a war cry, I fling the paint in their direction. It explodes outwards in a wave of white, but I wasn't anticipating the weight of it, so it also drags the can out of my hand. That flies in their direction as well, and I watch in surprise as it soars straight at the driver's head, hitting him with such force that his eyes roll into the back of his skull and he drops to the ground like a sack of shit. I couldn't have planned it better if I tried.

I'm momentarily stunned, but the girls' cheers draw my attention, and I look to the other kidnapper. The paint covering his face has blinded him. In his surprise, he releases the clip in his gun again, and it drops to the ground. He follows it down, scrambling around to find it, the paint hampering his efforts.

While he's distracted, I grab the shovel from the back of the van, then I channel my inner Xena Warrior Princess and go all gangsta on his ass, smacking him in the back of the head. He collapses face-first into the dirt, out cold.

Breathing heavily, I lean on the shovel to catch my breath and gain my bearings. "I'd make a damn good bounty hunter, and not just because of my tits and ass."

Dropping the shovel, I gesture to the girls and help them climb out of the van. I turn to survey where we are and notice a cabin off to the side. There doesn't seem to be any other cars. I press my finger to my mouth to tell the girls to be quiet as we approach the cabin carefully. The steps up to the door creak as we cross them. I peer in through the small window in the door. The interior looks to be a single room, and it's empty of people. Turning the handle and pushing the door open, I gesture for the girls to stay out while I have a look. They both seem unsure but listen and remain where they are.

I tiptoe into the room and look around. It's quite obvious no one else is here. "Girls, come inside quickly."

They enter, and I close the door and lock it, but

then rethink my plan and open the door. "Stay here," I tell them and run back to the unconscious kidnappers.

I roll over the man I hit with the paint can. His nose is bleeding, but his eyelids start to flutter, and a groan leaves his mouth as I search his pockets. I'm looking for the keys to the van, but he must have left them in the ignition, and he's waking up too quickly for me to look for them.

Grabbing his phone, I jump back and fall onto my ass as he makes a sloppy grab at my hand. Luckily, he's still disorientated. Climbing to my feet, I pull my foot back and give him an almighty kick in the balls. His face contorts with agony, and he clasps his hands over his nether regions as he rolls over and vomits into the dirt.

"You fucking bitch," he rasps. "When I get my hands on you—oof."

I step on his back as I move to grab the gun he lost off to the side. I swiftly head over to the other man I knocked on the head with a shovel and grab his weapon and the lost clip. He's also starting to come around, and I don't have time to search his pockets.

Taking the phone and the two guns, I race back to the cabin, where I slam the door shut behind me and turn the lock. I toss the phone and weapons onto a little coffee table before turning to study the lock. It doesn't look very sturdy. Nearby is an old-fashioned, rolltop desk. I try to push it toward the door, but it's so massive that even with my enhanced demon strength, it moves slowly. What is this thing made of?

I almost get it there when there's a giant crash against the door, and it shudders, bowing inwards as the latch rattles with the force. The girls scream in fright, and they both run over to me. Together, we get the desk positioned in front of the door, making entry into the cabin difficult. Looking around, I find another couple of windows, but they have bars in them, so they won't be able to come through there.

I collapse back onto the small sofa, and a whoosh of air escapes my lungs. Wiping the sweat from my brow, I push away a couple of tendrils of hair that are sticking to my face. Both girls cuddle next to me, and I just breathe. The adrenaline rush is starting to leave my body, and I'm beginning to shake. Tears gather in my eyes, but I hold them back, not wanting to frighten the girls.

Leaning forward, I grab the phone I took and swipe the screen. My hope is shattered when the passcode screen comes up. Damn it! It's password protected. I try a couple of obvious ones, like pressing zero six times. Wrong. I push one, two, three, four, five, six. Also wrong. Huffing in disgust, I throw it back onto the table in defeat and study the guns. If I really have to, I could probably use one to defend us, but I'm going to leave them where they are unless I get desperate.

Another crash against the door has us all jumping, and a little scream escapes Zoe's mouth.

I hug them to me. "Okay, girls, it's okay. We're just going to sit here until they get bored or Daddy finds us." This time, there's another crash against the door, and the lock splinters and the door opens slightly, but the desk holds. They must have both hit it with their bodies. If they do it a few more times, then they are going to open it.

Looking around the one-room cabin, I search for somewhere to hide the girls. There's a bed in the back corner.

I look underneath it. It's dusty but big enough for them to hide. I gesture for them to come over, and then I tell them, "Climb under here and stay there until I tell you to come out."

Aria grabs my hand. "No, Mom, it's not safe. Stay here with us."

I give her a kiss on the cheek. "Aria, honey, I'm the adult, and I need you to look after Zoe while I'm looking after both of you. Can you do that for me, my precious girl?"

She looks at me, her face serious and solemn, but nods her head.

I give her another kiss before giving one to Zoe. "I'm so proud of both my brave girls."

They crawl under the bed, and I pull down the valance to cover them up, rolling my eyes. I know it's the most obvious place, but at least it's something.

While we were doing that, the banging against the door stopped. When I go back over to the small window and look out, I can see both of them sitting on the steps, looking a little worse for wear, and I listen to their conversation.

"Fucking hell, she's a menace," a voice growls.

This brings a small smile to my lips. They haven't seen anything yet. My stomach rumbles in hunger, and I look around the cabin. In the corner opposite the bed is a tiny kitchenette. Going over, I open one of the cupboards. There are a few cans of beans and things. I close it and open another, finding a box of granola bars. Grabbing three, I return to the bed and slide two under.

"I'm sorry, that's all I could find."

Two little voices thank me, and then I stand up, open mine, and wander back to the small window to continue eavesdropping while munching on my snack. Let's see what kind of information I can uncover.

"What are we going to do? The contract was just for the girls," one of the guys says, but their backs are to me, and I can't tell which one.

"Damn it, Chuck, don't you think I know that? When I get my hands on that bitch, I'm going to fuck her up. I think my nose is broken, and she kicked my balls into my throat. They are still throbbing."

Okay, so Chuck is the passenger, not the driver.

"Hand me your phone, that bitch took mine."

I see Chuck reach into a pocket and hand the other guy his phone.

He swipes his finger across the screen a couple of times and holds it to his ear. "Yeah, it's Randy. We got the fucking girls, but there's a problem. There was a woman with them, and we had to take her too." His head ducks, and he holds the phone away from his ear.

Whoever he's talking to must be yelling.

He listens and turns to look at Chuck. "You want me to what? No way! I didn't agree to anything like that. I might want to hurt the bitch, but I'm not going to kill her."

Holy crap, my pulse accelerates again. Kill me?

He continues to talk. "Yeah, okay, we'll wait until you get here." He must hang up because he starts talking to Chuck. "The boss is on the way to take care of the problem."

I watch as Chuck turns to look at the door, and I duck down so he can't see me.

"What are we going to do about her? How are we going to tell the boss that she got the drop on us and locked herself in the cabin? This is a mess, Randy. I didn't sign up for this, and now the boss wants to kill her." Standing up, he paces back and forth in front of the cabin. He has managed to somehow wipe most of the paint from his face, but his shirt is stuck to his body.

Randy stands up and stares at me through the window. "Listen, bitch, I don't want to be involved in any murder. Here's what we're going to do. We're going to get in our van and drive away. We're going to disappear for a while, and you aren't going to say anything about us. The boss is the one you want anyway. You keep quiet about us, you hear?" His head cocks to the side, and he waits for me to answer.

I think about it then nod my head. I want to know who's behind this and why. "Okay, but you have to leave me the shovel. Put it on the porch when you leave, and no warning your boss that I'm armed. I don't want to die, and you don't want me to, and I need to defend myself from the boss."

"I don't fucking care. We're out of here. We won't say anything to the boss." Neither of them wait for an answer.

I watch them hurry to the van. Chuck picks up the shovel and runs it back to the cabin while Randy slams the side door closed. They get into the cab, and the van roars to life, then in a cloud of dust, it quickly turns and heads back down the dirt drive, fishtailing in its hurry to leave.

I watch until the dust starts to settle, ensuring they are not returning, before I relax and begin to plan for the mastermind.

Chapter Sixteen

It doesn't take long to take stock of everything in the cabin. It's minimalistic at best, but a search through the cupboards reveals a few things. A little cabinet next to the bed produces a bottle of baby powder, some razor blades, and a small desk fan. Out of the kitchen cupboard comes five bottles of maple syrup—I'm not sure why you would need five, but I'm not complaining—and the cans of beans. I grab a feather pillow off the bed, and leaning up against a wall is a fishing rod, tackle box, and a lantern. I pull off the fishing line and grab a packet of tiny little ball bearing sinkers out of the tackle box. There must be at least a hundred of them.

Piling all my finds on the little coffee table, I call the girls out from under the bed for a break. I'm not sure how long we're going to have to wait. Maybe Nolan will get here before the mastermind, but I really don't want to get my hopes up and have them dashed, so I better be prepared.

I ignore the guns for now. Yeah, one could probably end the conflict quickly, but if the boss has their own weapon and starts shooting as well, I don't want to put the girls at risk of being hit by a stray bullet. Channeling my best MacGyver/Charlie's Angel, I plan some booby traps.

Again, the girls and I use all our muscles to move the rolltop desk back where it was initially. Once it's out of the way, the door swings open, the latch busted by the force of the kidnappers banging against it. Oh well, there's nothing we can do now, and we want the boss to enter the cabin.

Going outside, I walk around the cabin to examine what I'm working with. Out back is an outhouse, and next to that is a little shed. It's filled with various tools and junk, but it has nothing much in the way of weapons except for shovels and things, and I already have one of those.

For safety's sake, I decide that the girls can hide in there until I deal with the boss. Returning to the house, I grab the lantern and some of the blankets off the bed and take them back to the shed, where I make the girls a nest. They follow and watch what I'm doing.

"This is going to keep you safe and out of the way. I want you to stay here until I come and get you. Maybe you can tell each other stories or play a game of eye spy. I need you both to be brave."

They argue a little, but both agree to hide if they can help me set up the booby traps. I reluctantly agree, and they follow me back out to help.

On the side of the cabin is a hose. I pull it around to the front and ask the girls to make the ground wet and muddy just in front of the steps. With great concentration, her tongue poking out between her lips, Aria operates the hose while Zoe points out the bits she missed. They bicker the whole time, but a smile crosses my lips. They are distracted and unafraid for the moment.

While they do that, I tie the fishing line across the second step to the cabin. It's set down low, so no one should see it as they climb up, especially if they are distracted by the mud before it.

Once the girls are finished, they put the hose back, and I take them to the shed.

"Thank you for your help, but I need you to hide now. It can't be much longer before the bad people arrive." Giving them both a kiss and a hug, I help them into their nest. Their eyes are filled with tears, but they swallow down the fright and climb in together, snuggling close.

"Now, remember you have to be quiet. If you hear the door open, you need to stay very still and not make a sound."

After they nod their agreement, I cover them up. As I walk out of the shed, I look back, but it isn't apparent that two little girls are hiding under the blankets. With worry, I leave them, because it's all I can do now to protect them.

I return to the cabin, avoiding the mud and fishing line, and pick up the shovel Chuck left behind for me. I go inside and leave it there, then I grab the ball bearing sinkers and scatter them across the cabin porch. Phase one is complete. If they aren't disoriented and distracted by the time they get to the door, I'm not sure what we'll do, but fingers crossed it'll work.

Closing the door as far as it will go, I grab a pot from under the sink and pour maple syrup into it. I pull a chair over to the door, crack it open, and use the chair to place the pot on the door, off-center and leaning slightly against the doorframe to ensure it will fall forward, soaking whoever comes through.

Dragging the chair back a bit, I place it in front of the door. I pull the second one behind it then set the fan on the seat and plug it into a nearby socket. Going into the kitchen, I find a knife and start shredding the pillow, putting all the feathers on the chair in front of the fan. Once I finish, I grab the shovel, set it next to me, and take a seat on the sofa.

I'm exhausted from all the adrenaline rushes, and my energy is at an all-time low. I don't think I could conjure a tissue if I needed it. Thank goodness for my obsession with old movies and TV series.

I lean back to close my eyes just for a minute, trying to catch my breath.

I'm not sure how much time passes before the sound of a car on the gravel driveway wakes me from my doze. My heart rate ramps up, and nerves and anticipation kick my adrenaline into overdrive. Standing up, I wipe my sweaty palms on my jeans and stretch my tired body out. It's go time. I want to have a look at who's coming, but I need to sit behind the fan to turn it on.

I crouch down low behind the chair to make myself less visible while I wait. I can hear voices, but they are indistinguishable. *Come on, what are they doing?* My muscles start to complain, and pulsing bites of pain arc through my calves and thighs before I finally hear something.

"Where are those two idiots? Where's the van?" The man sounds irritated.

They don't sound like they are coming any closer. *Crap.* I hear a murmured reply, but I can't make out what the other person said.

"Well, if they went to get food, one of them better still be in there. Look, the door's cracked open." More murmuring. "If he's taking a shit, he better hurry up. Come on, let's get on with this." The man sounds pissed off.

They must both step into the mud at the same time, because I hear swearing and exclamations of annoyance. Is that a woman's voice I hear? Before I can overthink it, a sequence of events occurs. They both trip on the fishing wire, then the sinkers continue to unbalance them, and the cursing gets louder. The scraping of shoes and the loud thuds of unstable footsteps also ring through the cabin.

I'm sure if someone could see me now, the wicked grin on my face would be scary.

"What the fuck is this?"

Before I can blink, the door bangs open, and like a slow-motion camera shot, I watch in shock and surprise as the maple syrup bucket drops, covering Bridgette and her lawyer in five liters of maple syrup. The pot hits the lawyer on the head, and like Randy before him, he falls to the ground, knocked unconscious by the force.

Huh, wasn't sure if that would work or not.

A screech leaves Bridgette's mouth, but before she can do anything, I quickly flip the switch on the fan. As the blades reach top speed, fluffy white feathers fly toward her like heat-seeking missiles. She immediately gets covered, the feathers sticking to the maple syrup still dripping down her body.

Coughing and spluttering, she starts spewing threats. "When I get my hands on you, bitch, I'm going to make you suffer. Taking my man and my children and my money. You stole my lif—"

The clang of the shovel smacking her in the face is music to my ears. The feathers and syrup must have blocked her view, or she didn't think I would come after her, because the woman didn't even flinch when I swung.

"No, bitch, you did that all yourself, and they are *my* men and *my* kids."

The sound of her body hitting the ground is muffled as her lawyer breaks her fall. The gun in her hand, which I hadn't noticed, clatters to the floor next to her.

Shit, she really was serious about killing me.

I run back to the bed and grab another blanket out of the box next to it. Laying it down on the floor, I roll Bridgette and her lawyer onto it. Next, I search through their pockets, pulling out Bridgette's phone and the keys for the lawyer's car. Folding the blanket across their bodies, I bundle them up like a Christmas present before wrapping fishing line around the blanket, running it up and down the length. I use the whole spool before tying it off. If they wake up before we are rescued, neither of them will be able to get very far.

Rolling the package like a sausage, I push them out the door. The sound of lead sinkers rolling across the porch in my wake reminds me to be careful where I step. I pull my foot back, and with a kick, the unconscious bundle tumbles down the steps. Wincing, I watch as both of their heads smack together on the way down.

Ha, that's going to leave a bruise.

Just to make sure that they don't get any ideas if they wake up, I run around to the side and take the hose off the tap, and then I add it as another layer, securing them tighter than a teenager in skinny jeans.

Finally finished, I sit back down on the steps, huffing out a breath and wiping the sweat from my brow. I shake my head as I study the lump. The poor girls. I don't think I'll tell them. Their mother's a real piece of work.

Heading back into the cabin, I grab the shovel, the phone, keys, and a glass of water then return to the front to sit on the steps. My stomach rumbles, the sound loud in the silence of the wooded area. Taking a sip of water to soothe my dry throat, I examine the phone, but like the other one, this is also passcode protected. I throw it at the couple in my disgust, and it bounces off the blanketed bundle and lands in the mud. Shrugging my shoulders, I decide to leave it there. It's not like they are going to need it when they wake up.

After I finish my water, I grab the keys and use the remote to pop the trunk of the car when a faint sound draws my attention. I look toward the driveway as the noise gets louder. Through the trees, I see blue and red flashing lights.

The wailing sirens get louder, and dust rises in the wake of the police car and pimped-out SUV flying down the driveway. The police lights reflect off the dust, which hovers in the air before slowly dissipating. I watch with interest as the cars come to a screeching halt beside the lawyer's car. Five men jump out of the cop car and SUV with their guns drawn.

Standing up, I put my hands on my hips and prop one foot on the bundled kidnappers. "Well, it's about damn time. Luckily I'm no damsel in distress. I'm the hero of this story."

The two cops come to a halt, and their expressions of shock are laughable. The other three men don't stop, but they do lower their guns before they surround me. I don't know how they manage it, but all three wrap their arms around me at the same time, squeezing me tight as they cover me in kisses. Their jumble of voices is reassuring and comforting, and for the first time since the van pulled up at the park, I'm able to relax.

The relief I feel at seeing them brings all my emotions to the surface, and I promptly burst into tears.

Chapter Seventeen

After giving me plenty of kisses and wiping my tears away, the guys pull back and look me over to reassure themselves that I'm okay.

"Glory, where are the girls?" Nolan asks, looking around with a panicked, worried expression on his face.

"They are hiding in the shed out back," I tell him, pointing to the rear of the cabin. He turns to leave, but I lunge forward and grab his arm. "Um, just wait a second, will you? I don't want them to see this."

He looks at me with confusion on his face.

As one, the four of us turn back toward the cops. They have managed to remove the hose and fishing line and are finally unwrapping the blanket to reveal the culprits.

"Fuck," Carter growls.

"Is that…" Louis trails off, his French accent thick with emotion.

"You have got to be kidding me!" Nolan brushes past us and heads toward the two people still lying on the ground.

Louis and Carter jump forward and hold him back.

"Let me go!" he shouts at them, struggling. "I'm going to kill the bitch."

I step in front of him, grabbing his chin and forcing him to look at me. "Nolan, stop!" I demand. "She's not getting out of this. Don't do anything you'll regret, please," I beg.

The anger in his eyes fades, and he nods his head, dragging me close and holding me.

We watch as the cops place handcuffs on them both. The lawyer, whose name I can't remember, has a bump on his forehead the size of an orange. That pot must have been more substantial than I thought to cause that kind of damage.

Giggling quietly, I turn to look at Bridgette and smile in satisfaction. Unlike the polished, stylish woman who came to our door, she is a mess. Her dark hair looks like a bird made a nest in it. When I rolled them, she must have gathered things as she went. It has feathers, sticks, and mud in it. Her nose has to be broken, and she has two black eyes. Not only that, but when she opens her mouth, it's bloody and painful looking. I may have knocked out a few teeth, or at least loosened them.

Neither of them protest much as the cops read them their rights and help them into the back of the police car. One cop climbs into the driver's side, but the other makes his way back to me.

"Ma'am, we need you to come down to the station and give your version of events, please."

Nodding my head, I gesture back to the cabin. "You'll find a couple of guns in there. I didn't touch the one on the ground, but the two on the coffee table will probably have my prints on them. They came off the other guys."

Drawing his gun, the cop looks around in confusion. "What other guys? Where are they?"

"At ease, soldier," I say sarcastically. "They were smart enough to get out of Dodge while they had the chance, but I can give you a description and a plate number."

He holsters his gun and relaxes slightly. "Alright, come down to the station as soon as you can." He turns to Nolan. "I'm relying on you to get her there."

Nolan nods his assent, and the cop retrieves the weapons, putting them into evidence bags before getting into the passenger side. With flashing lights, they disappear down the driveway again, kicking more dust into the air.

"Thank God the trash has been taken out." I sigh as we watch them disappear into the woods. "Come on." I grab Nolan's hand, and with Carter and Louis following us, we run to the little shed out back, slamming open the door and calling the girls' names.

They both poke their heads out of their little nest, and their eyes light up when Nolan shoves me out of the way. Smiling, I watch as he throws himself at them, pulling them close and covering them with kisses. Carter and Louis squeeze past me as well and join the pile. The love in my heart swells even more as I see my family back together and safe again.

After rescuing the girls from the shed, we pile into the big black SUV and drive home. The girls, obviously feeling better now that they are safe from harm, keep the guys entertained with the story of our ordeal. As it turns out, the trail of crap I threw out the van window is what helped them find us. Someone saw me doing it, called the police, and reported it, and the guys were at the police station reporting our kidnapping after they'd received the photo of me and the girls from my phone. They found the abandoned car and my smashed phone, and had gone straight to the police. They joined the chase when the cops went to investigate, because all three just had a strange feeling it was me.

When we get home, I take a quick shower, and Louis prepares me a meal while I wash up. I eat until I feel like I'm going to pop. The whole thing has left me feeling wrung out, and all I want to do is curl up in my bed with my mates, but that will have to wait. While Nolan takes care of the girls, Carter and Louis run me to the police station to make my statement.

They both sit and hold my hands for two hours as I go over the whole ordeal. I tell them about Chuck and Randy and how they both got cold feet when a phone call to their boss, the person who hired them to kidnap the girls, turned into something a little more than they bargained for.

The police, Carter, and Louis all have a great laugh as I tell them about the way I had gotten the better of Chuck and Randy. I give them a description of them both, a license plate number, and a description of the van. I don't think it will take much to find them. They didn't seem all that smart to start with, though they'll probably be offered plea deals for testifying against Bridgette and her lawyer.

As for Bridgette, her lawyer is singing like a canary. He only had a slight concussion and was released to police custody. Bridgette is a little worse for wear and is being kept in the hospital for observation overnight, handcuffed to a bed. Her nose needs to be set, and a dentist needs to look at her loose teeth.

The lawyer says it was all her idea. He confirmed she'd run out of money. When the plan to try for custody was thrown out, she was furious and planned the kidnapping. She was hoping to ransom the girls for a significant amount, knowing that Nolan would do anything for them. My growl of disgust is echoed by both Louis and Carter at the thought that the biological mother of those beautiful girls cared so little for them and they were just a means to an end.

When she received the phone call from Randy about me, she was practically giddy with joy. She saw it as an opportunity to take care of the other problem—me. The lawyer told the cops that she had every intention of putting a bullet in my brain and hadn't cared that she would scar the girls for life.

God, I'm glad we left Nolan at home. The three of us agree he probably doesn't need to know that bit, because it would just make him feel worse.

Finally, we're allowed to leave after being reassured that Bridgette wouldn't see the light of day for a long time and would probably be someone's bitch very soon. On the drive home, the guys tell me again about how they'd received the anonymous text that we now realize must have come from Bridgette's or the lawyer's phone. That must have been who Randy had sent the photo he took of us to. They also told me about how Nolan's wrath demon had lost control when they got to the park and found the abandoned car, picnic blanket, and backpack. Apparently, there wasn't much left of the tree that we'd set the blanket under once he'd taken out his frustration, his wrath demon at full capacity due to the situation.

Resting my head on the window, I feel my eyes start to close. The sound of the guys murmuring to each other lulls me into a restless sleep. Visions of Randy and Chuck flash through my mind, as does Bridgette's sneer and the girls' frightened, tear-stained faces. I can feel my body twitch, since I'm not in a deep sleep but not quite awake either.

The car rolls to a stop, and the doors open and close, drawing me further out of my nightmares. A pair of arms wrap around me as someone carries me, finally waking me enough to open my eyes and look around. The rooms and walls move past as Carter brings me upstairs to our bedroom. Louis leads the way, opening the door, and Carter strides in. Nolan is already there with his shirt off. He's sitting up in bed with a book in his hand, and a relieved smile crosses his face as Carter sets me down next to him. Putting the book down, he snuggles closer to me as I watch Louis and Carter both strip down.

Nolan helps me remove my clothes, and when he pulls my shirt over my head, he draws my attention away from the other two.

Cupping his face, I place a kiss on his lips. "How are the girls?" I ask him quietly.

"They are okay," he tells me, looking a little sad. "They are in the same bed tonight, and I had to leave the door all the way open. They wouldn't let me leave until they fell asleep, but I think they'll be okay. They kept talking about how brave their mommy was and how they both hope to be as brave as you when they grow up. I think that's part of the reason they haven't joined us in here. They want to be just like Mommy."

My heart melts, and tears well in my eyes. I feel so much love. Warm hands settle on my body, and I turn my head. Louis has slid in behind me, spooning me from behind, and Carter has snuggled in behind Louis.

Nolan reaches over and squeezes them both before his hands drift back to rest on my body. The light goes out, and the stress of the day finally leaves. I slip into a deep sleep without dreams, wrapped safely in my men's arms.

Acknowledgments

To Jen, Kandi, Serena, Lucy, Kelly and Emma, the wonderful woman I shared the Leaving Eden Anthology with, which Glory was originally a part of. Thank you for all your help and support through the process. It gave me the confidence I needed to take the leap to publish my solo books.

Thank you Claire for your shared knowledge and your patience with my formatting dramas. You are an inspiration and I want to be just like you when I grow up.

Thank you to Jillian Locke for her invaluable proof reading eyes, you re awesome.

I had a blast writing Glory originally and I just couldn't get her to be quiet, her story had to finish. And who knows we may still see more of Glory in the future. Keep an eye out on my facebook group for future updates.

Lexie